# Tangled REVERENCE

BEST SELLING AUTHOR
# DARIE McCOY

Edited by: All That's Wright

Cover Art/Design: Covers In Color

Inside Title Page: Covers In Color

EBook ISBN: 978-1-7390363-6-2

Print ISBN: 978-1-7390363-7-9

# Preacher's Kid Series

Experience the passionate whirlwind of emotions and the tender exploration of faith as the Preacher's Kids confront their past, embrace their present, and unlock the door to their hearts. Each story is a captivating journey filled with heat, passion, and a revelation of love that will leave you spellbound.

*For those of us who are still finding our way through the uncharted streets of adulthood.*

# Prologue

Pastor Atarah Cox stood behind the lectern in the pulpit of the church she dearly loved, allowing her gaze to travel over the assembled members of the congregation. Her message this Sunday was designed to convict, but also remind the membership of their first duty as believers—being helpers. So, she'd preached from the Gospel According to Matthew. Specifically, on the topic surrounding why Jesus entered the temple, turned over tables, evicting the money changers, and all others who were doing business inside.

When her eyes landed on Cyrus Lauder, she noticed the firm set of his jaw beneath his neatly trimmed beard. Even if she hadn't, the rigidity in his shoulders as he sat ramrod straight in the pew was hard to miss. Unlike some of the parishioners who were visibly squirming, he was stock-still. No. He wasn't uncomfortable. He was angry. His cognac-colored eyes appeared darker as they flashed with his discontent.

Good. It was no more than he deserved for what he'd pulled with the board, luring the majority of votes to his side in favor of selling the property she wanted to renovate to further their community outreach. Smugness was unbecoming, but Atarah felt it welling inside her as she regarded the results of her convicting sermon. It was one which would've made her daddy proud.

That is, if he was still speaking to her after her refusal to give up on being the pastor of her own church to settle for being a first lady and head of the Deaconess Board. Shaking away the unpleasant thought, Atarah wrapped up as normal, before going to her position at the door to shake hands as people exited the church.

She was feeling pretty good about herself when she entered her office to remove her robe and gather her things to leave. There weren't any other activities planned for the day. So, she was looking forward to stopping by her cousin's house for Sunday dinner. Iva had sent her a message saying she was cooking Atarah's favorite. Pork chops smothered in gravy, cabbage, sweet corn with cornbread sounded so amazing her stomach rumbled in anticipation.

As she turned from placing her robe into the closet, her breath caught in her throat. Cyrus stood framed in her doorway. His nostrils flared with his deep inhale as he stepped over the threshold, closing the door behind him.

Lifting one eyebrow, Atarah closed the closet door and stood in front of it with her arms folded. Waiting.

"Just what was that all about?" Cyrus's normally deep voice sounded like someone had scraped sandpaper over his vocal cords.

"Good afternoon to you too, Mr. Lauder." Unfolding her arms, Atarah crossed the room to her desk. Her reference to him as Mr. instead of Brother was purposeful. "I'm not sure I understand what you're talking about."

"You know d—" Cutting off the likely curse, Cyrus squared his shoulders and lowered his voice. "You know exactly what I'm talking about. It was no coincidence you decided to teach that particular lesson today after what happened with the Lloyd property this past week. You did it just to goad me."

Sniffing, Atarah reached into the left-hand bottom drawer of the desk to remove her purse. Even after no longer working in the corporate world, she wasn't able to break the habit of storing it there.

"I know it's hard for you to believe, but I don't structure my sermons around you. I wouldn't deign to try to diminish your importance. But everything isn't about you, Cyrus Lauder."

It was good the Lord didn't see fit to strike people down for lying on church grounds, because she would've had a lightning bolt to the ass for that one.

"It's funny you should call it a lesson rather than a sermon though. Is it because you actually learned something today? Could it be you now understand the concept of ministry?"

Looking down at her purse, she dug inside to locate her keys. She had no intention of entertaining him a moment longer. President of the church board or not, he didn't get to just show up in her office trying to chastise her about what she preached. Warmth hit her back before she was whipped around by Cyrus's hold on her upper arm.

"Excuse you! I know you didn't just put your hands on me!"

Atarah really wished the heat flooding her body could be totally attributed to anger, but it would be as big a lie as when she told Cyrus her sermon wasn't aimed at him. His light brown eyes were shooting daggers; however, she held his gaze with fire in her own.

Removing his hand from her arm as if direct contact with her skin burned him, Cyrus leaned closer to her. He was no longer physically holding on to her, but his big body kept her trapped between him and the sturdy wooden desk.

"Don't do that." When he finally spoke, he didn't bother to address his handsy behavior.

Atarah's frown was pointed as she returned his glare. "Don't do what? And is it necessary for you to be this close to me? You'd never treat a male pastor this way."

"I wouldn't have to explain to a male pastor why we shouldn't throw money at a derelict building. *He* would understand how fiscally irresponsible it is to use the church funds that way."

Atarah's jaw dropped. The nerve of this Neanderthal. This pompous misogynist. Putting a hand up, she pressed against his chest, trying to create space between them.

"You know what? You are completely out of line, not to mention rude. I'm *not* having this discussion with you. I said what needed to be said at the meeting. If you can't handle a mirror being held up to your actions, maybe pray about it or seek therapy. Either way, this conversation is over."

Ignoring her bid for space, Cyrus maintained his posture. Initially, Atarah was just irritated. After all, they bumped heads regularly. But, he was taking things too far this time. Pressing both hands to his chest, she used more strength to shove him back.

He didn't move. Not an inch. However, what did happen was her hands were trapped beneath his, right before his lips came crashing down on hers. *What the hell?* Her shock was swiftly eclipsed by the heat blazing beneath her skin.

He tasted better than she'd imagined. Even though she regretted it afterwards, she'd had more than one fantasy about Cyrus Lauder and the possible talents he had with the tongue currently tangling with hers.

"Oh! Pastor! Brother Lauder! I didn't—I mean—Oh my!" Celia's jumbled words trailed off as Cyrus snatched away from Atarah.

Atarah's fingers were still aloft when he backed away. The separation was so swift, she nearly toppled over, because she hadn't realized she'd begun to lean on him during their kiss. In the split second it took her to fully comprehend what happened, Celia had already turned away. The slamming door was like a bucket of ice water being poured over Atarah's head.

*What had she done?*

# Chapter One

Cyrus stood looking at his reflection in the mirror at the estate he'd secured for the day's activities. His bespoke tuxedo was cut to perfection. The insinuation that he wouldn't be able to get what he wanted in such a short time frame was laughable. As his grandfather had taught him in more ways than one, money talks.

So, he was dressed to marry his bride in the suit he'd chosen from the local designer who'd been making big waves, providing menswear for the athletes, actors and society elite. The man had even shown up to make any last-minute alterations that may have been necessary.

"Do you plan to stand there staring at yourself for the rest of the day, or are we going outside?"

Cyrus looked over his shoulder at his brother, Caleb. Wearing an almost identical suit, his brother stood next to the full-length mirror with his shoulder propped against one wall.

"Stand up straight, Caleb. You'll ruin the lines of the suit. And, no. I don't plan to simply stare at myself. We'll go out there when it's time."

"Are you hiding from your future wife?"

Identical cognac-colored eyes met his when Cyrus shot his brother a glare. He neither confirmed nor denied his brother's taunting words. As his younger sibling was the only member of his family present, he didn't punch him in the face for implying he would want to hide from his bride. Instead, Cyrus simply stared at him until Caleb did as he'd directed and stood up straight.

Tugging on his cuffs, then the bottom of his suit jacket, Caleb's lips tilted up on one side.

"Happy now? All straightened out. No damage."

As he walked away, Cyrus heard him mumbling about the suit not being a rental, and he could do what he wanted with his own property. Cyrus wouldn't allow himself to be goaded though. Doing that is what got him into this situation to begin with.

### *Four Months Earlier*

*The second Cyrus heard Celia's voice, he knew whatever happened next wouldn't be good. As much as he didn't want to, he pulled away from Atarah. Despite popular opinion, he did respect her position as pastor, but in his head and heart he didn't call her by the title, because it put more distance between them. Distance that had to be there for them to continue to function in their roles at Harmony Haven.*

*He couldn't stop himself from gathering her in his arms again when she nearly toppled over after he abruptly released her. Celia was already on her way out of the door, so she didn't see it. But, it wouldn't matter. The damage had been done. He, more than anyone, knew how quickly the information would go from the secretary's lips to the ears of the church leadership. Damnit.*

*The stricken expression covering Atarah's face was confirmation of her awareness of the clusterfuck they now found themselves in. The two of them together in a non-platonic capacity, was a conflict of interest. For people in their position, the only way for a relationship to happen was for one of them to step down from their role.*

*There was no way on this side of heaven Atarah would walk away from being a pastor. Not after essentially being disowned by her parents for yielding to her calling. For different reasons, he couldn't vacate his position as the president of the church board. It was his business savvy, which allowed them to afford the hefty salaries of not just the pastor, but the other paid positions within Harmony Haven.*

*They could possibly manage without him, however standing on the sidelines wasn't exactly his strong suit. So, what were they to do? By the time Celia was done, the congregation would likely believe he'd followed through on the desire he hadn't acted on and had Atarah's dress nearly ripped from her body.*

*"You realize she's going to tell everyone she crosses paths with what she just saw. We both know Celia plays fast and loose with the details."*

*Atarah's head dropped for a second before she looked back up at him. "I know. We've had more than one conversation about it. I was on the verge of re-assigning her, but I probably won't be able to do that now. H—"*

*Catching herself, she cut the word off before she cursed. When she started again, she inserted a replacement word for the one it was obvious she wanted to use. "Heck... I'll be lucky to have a job this time next week."*

*Rubbing her arms, Cyrus shook his head. "Uh-uh. Don't do that. They'd run me off before they asked you to step down. More than half of the congregation would leave if you left."*

*The assurances fell from his lips easily, because they were true. The membership hung on Atarah's every word. Her acceptance of each person, no matter what, had endeared her to the diverse congregation of their non-denominational church. No matter how often they were at odds about the correct way to manage the church when it came to properties and expenditures, he couldn't withhold what he knew to be true.*

*Her dark chocolate eyes regarded him with wonder for a moment. They darted away once she realized their current position, with her being encircled by his arms. This time, when she pressed against his chest in a bid to gain more space, he actually moved. Placing slightly more than an arm's length between them, he stared at her.*

*He didn't like the way her shoulders slumped nor the dejection in her expression. They'd both grown up in the church with pastors for fathers—although different denominations. And, while Harmony Haven had broken away from many of the traditional Christian church norms, some things they held fast to.*

*Their very single pastor being caught in a lover's embrace with a member of the church board would blaze through the congregation like a wildfire. The only way to stop it was to get in front of it.*

*"I don't want you to worry about this. I'll handle it. Go on about your day as you planned. I'll call you tomorrow."*

*Unlike the numerous times when he'd decisively stated his stance or opinions to her, Atarah didn't argue or push back in the slightest. Almost in a daze, she picked up her purse, grabbed her overcoat from the hook next to the door and walked out of the office. She didn't even bother to make him leave so she could lock the door behind her.*

### *Present*

As he turned away from his reflection, Cyrus wondered how Atarah was feeling. He didn't hope for the giddy anticipation he'd heard most brides felt. At best, he prayed he didn't walk outside just to learn she'd run away. It wasn't like she'd been enthusiastic about his suggestion they get married with the board's approval.

Her exact words were that he was *out of his rabid ass mind*. And of course, she said it while wearing one of her favorite tee shirts. The eggshell blue, wide neck shirt had the phrase, I love Jesus, but I cuss a little, scrawled across the front. Cyrus still felt like the words, *a little*, should be replaced by *a lot*. Because that's how it seemed to him.

Although he wasn't one to talk. He wasn't a stranger to using colorful language, as his mother called it. When the thought of his mother flit across his mind, Cyrus reflexively rubbed the area above his heart. As if he knew the turn of his brother's thoughts, Caleb laid a hand on his shoulder.

"Hey, we both know why she's not here. Try not to let it get to you. You're about to marry an amazing, beautiful woman who has more genuine kindness in her than the entirety of the place we came from."

Despite his tendency to be a smartass, Caleb knew exactly what to say. Until he went and kept talking.

"I still don't know how you convinced her to marry you. I could've sworn she hated you."

"Don't worry about the how. Just focus on the results." Shaking off the brief feelings of melancholy, Cyrus pinned his brother with a hard stare. "Do you have the rings?"

Patting his pocket, Caleb assured him, "right here, safe and sound."

Of course, Cyrus wasn't satisfied until Caleb pulled them out to show him. All this despite him knowing he'd placed the diamonds encircled with a platinum band in Caleb's hand less than two hours ago. But nothing, absolutely nothing, could stop this wedding from moving forward.

# Chapter Two

"Cuz, you know I'm with you no matter what. But, I know something's up. It's your wedding day, yet you're sitting over there staring out of the window like you want to be anywhere besides here."

"I'm fine, Iva. Really." Atarah was aware she didn't sound the least bit convincing, but her cousin didn't call her out on it.

Iva rubbed between Atarah's shoulder blades the way her mama used to when she wasn't feeling well as a little girl. The action didn't soothe Atarah as it had when she had a tummy ache at five. Instead, it reminded her of her parents' absence from what should be a joyous occasion in her life. Her marriage had been a long-held hope of her mother's. Atarah had been practically groomed from birth to be a wife, mother and first lady.

She was supposed to marry the minister of an upstanding Baptist church, then produce more little devout Christians to follow in their family footsteps of being good little soldiers in the army of salvation. Only, Atarah did the unacceptable. She sought to preach instead of standing behind the man proclaiming the word. The very idea was an abomination to her father. And what was intolerable to him was intolerable to his wife.

So, when they didn't show up for Atarah's graduation from seminary, she knew where she stood in their lives. Not having either of them here, when she was about to join her life with another's, hurt. Even if the marriage was a farce—a tool being used to keep her in the seat she'd earned, with the people she'd cultivated a relationship with.

It's possible she could've rolled the dice—given the congregation the opportunity to rally behind her. However, despite her popularity amongst the membership, she wasn't positive things would've gone her way. The rumor mill had her practically naked, making adult films in her office in a matter of hours after Celia burst in on the kiss she shared with Cyrus.

The lip lock was hot beyond anything she'd ever experienced, but her clothing hadn't burned off her body—even if it felt like it should have. She'd left the church in a daze and drove home in a fog. The delicious meal her cousin cooked was forgotten until Iva called her to find out why she hadn't arrived yet.

The Cox family was large while being small at the same time. They had a plethora of extended family. However, in the area, there were only a handful of them. Those who had faithfully attended her father's church treated Atarah like a leper. Iva, who hadn't drunk the same sweet elixir, was the family member who stood firm with her when the rest turned away.

Tearing her gaze from the beautifully decorated garden below, Atarah looked up at Iva, who remained standing next to her.

Pulling a smile up from her depths, she winked at her slightly older cousin.

"I promise, Iv. I'm fine. Seriously. It's just one of those things. I needed a minute to realize that once again the world hadn't ended because my parents chose not to support me."

Despite her reservations, she and Cyrus had sent them an invitation. Instead of an RSVP, they'd received it back with *Return to Sender* stamped on the outside of the envelope. If she wasn't sure of their position, that action made it abundantly clear.

"It's their loss, Rah-rah. They are going to regret this. I'd say sooner rather than later."

Iva's use of the childhood nickname brought a real smile to Atarah's face. Over the years, she moved from Rah-rah to just Rah. But, on occasion, Iva reverted to the original. It warmed Atarah's heart. She desperately needed it. She was battling with going through with the farce she'd let Cyrus talk her into.

Initially, he'd approached her with the option of going to the board and coming clean about their relationship. He brushed off her questioning, *what relationship*, to get to the second part of his plan where they'd then stage an amicable break up in a couple of weeks. The plan was a non-starter from the moment he voiced it. Having a secret relationship be *'discovered'* by the church secretary, then *'going public'* only to *'break up'* a short while later would've been far more damaging than simply telling the truth.

She shot his next plan down almost as quickly. Who was going to believe they'd been madly in love for more than a year? That their arguments, although real, hadn't stopped them from having a relationship in secret and wanting to get married. *No one.* At least it's what Atarah thought until she was standing next to Cyrus in the conference room with her hand clasped in his.

They fell for it. Every. Single. One of them. And she never said a word. She just let him talk. Let him offer solutions to remove the appearance of conflict of interest so they could both maintain their positions. He wouldn't be allowed to attend any meetings or have a direct vote when there were discussions regarding her compensation or future at the church. A few other fail safes were implemented to make certain he also didn't use his influence to benefit Atarah's position in any way.

That last condition she found laughable. They were rarely on the same side of an issue when it came to how to or if they should spend church funds. So, him using his influence to sway anyone to her side was unlikely to occur.

A knock on the door pulled Atarah back into the moment, drawing hers and Iva's attention.

"Come in." Atarah didn't ask who it was. It could only be one of two people—the wedding planner or her new church secretary, Norma. When the door opened, the wedding planner, Rita, poked her head into the room.

"We're all set. It's time to move you to the staging room."

Pasting a smile on her face once more, Atarah stood to follow the woman from the room. She wanted to chuckle at there being a staging area for such a small wedding. Iva, who was her only bridesmaid, was also serving as her maid of honor. There were also the flower girl and ring bearer. The only other member of the wedding party, aside from Cyrus and his brother Caleb, was the minister.

Cassius Hall was her mentor from seminary. He was more than happy to make the trip to Logan City to officiate. Although it ruffled a few feathers, she stood firm on the decision. Other than selecting her wedding dress, it was one of the few things she'd offered more than a minimum input on. She didn't have to.

Cyrus hired an excellent wedding planner who came with a wealth of ideas. All Atarah had to do was point and say yes or no to the options presented to her. She'd known he was wealthy, however the way he threw money at their impending nuptials said she'd miscalculated by at least a digit.

It wasn't loud. There was simply a hum of activity in the massive house they were using for the event. The size of the wedding party was small, but the number of attendees wasn't. They expected the majority of the congregation to attend. Once Rita had them ensconced in the designated staging room, she left them alone.

Iva stood at one of the windows, peeking outside through a sliver she created between the curtain and the edge of the window frame.

"Girl, how many people did y'all invite? Is this why you didn't have it at your church?"

Fixing the skirt of her dress so as not to wrinkle it, Atarah glanced up at her cousin.

"We invited the congregation. It would've been rude not to. Cyrus also invited some of his friends and business associates."

"What about you? Your friends?" Iva's lip twitched, then she stared at Atarah with one raised eyebrow.

Recognizing the expression, Atarah pursed her lips instead of sticking out her tongue like a four-year-old.

17

"I invited people too. You aren't my only friend."

Closing the curtain, Iva walked over to the settee where Atarah was seated, lowering herself on the other end.

"I never said I was your only friend. I was just the only one ready to stand up for you on the spur of the moment." Smoothing her hand along the hip flare of the canary yellow bridesmaid dress, she continued, "it didn't hurt to have Cyrus volunteer to foot the bill for my dress, shoes and accessories."

With a short shake of her head, Atarah cast a censuring glance at her favorite cousin and best friend.

"You are so wrong for that."

"Whatever." Iva flipped her hand in Atarah's general direction before patting the hair at her temples.

Hair which was styled to perfection courtesy of the session Cyrus purchased for both of them at Murphy's Salon and Spa. Neither of them was allowed to even tip the hair stylists when they were done. He'd taken care of all of it.

They were only in the room a little over five minutes before Rita was back at the door, ushering them out. Atarah's heartbeat accelerated with each step she took toward the opening. This was really happening. She'd come too far to turn back, but the light tremble of her digits made the bouquet Rita placed into her hands visibly shake.

This was it. She was really about to marry Cyrus Lauder. *Dear Lord...* Atarah sent up the silent prayer amidst her guilt at knowing she was about to walk out into that beautiful garden and commit to a lie.

# Chapter Three

Standing with his brother on his left with the minister on his right, Cyrus's gaze was glued to the French doors at the end of the white runner leading to the flower-covered arch. He anxiously awaited the appearance of his bride. The doors had been closed after flowers were strewn all over the runner by one of the little girls from the church.

Her mother was one of the assistants over the children's ministry. She was more than happy to volunteer her child for the role. Cyrus could admit the child looked adorable in her little white princess dress with canary yellow ribbon threaded through the lace along the bottom and at the puffy short sleeves. Similar colored flowers were woven into the floral crown she wore.

Watching her carefully toss the rose petals on the white runner, he experienced an unfamiliar tug on his heart. Squashing it, he redirected his stare to the people who'd accepted their invitation to attend their nuptials. Of the large crowd assembled, roughly thirty were people who weren't members of Harmony Haven.

The length of the constructed aisle had little to do with the size of their wedding party and everything to do with the number of people gathered to watch the two of them wed. Just when he thought he might have to go back inside to see what was taking so long, the garden doors swung open, revealing his bride.

Cyrus didn't realize he'd stopped breathing, until Caleb bumped his shoulder, whisper-shouting in his ear, commanding him to breathe. Releasing the air trapped in his lungs, Cyrus ate Atarah up with his gaze as she slowly moved closer. The beautiful ballad, being sung by the lead soloist from the choir, didn't filter into his ears, as his total focus was on his bride.

Walking alone, with her head high and a slight smile on her beautiful face, no one would ever guess she wasn't head over heels in love with him. As much as he visually devoured her, her chocolate-colored eyes were glued to his face. She looked neither left nor right, but directly at him. If he didn't know she was reluctant to agree to doing this, he would've been as convinced as everyone else she was a woman about to marry the love of her life.

*If only that were true.*

Atarah stopped at the bottom of the short stairs leading up to the small dais where he stood next to the minister and his brother. Atarah's cousin, Iva, stood to the other side of the minister while the children sat on a specially made bench nearby. It took every ounce of Cyrus's self-control to remain where he was until it was time to physically take her hand to bring her up to stand next to him.

Thankfully, Pastor Hall didn't dally. He spoke the first words to begin the ceremony.

"Dearly beloved, we are gathered here today…"

The rest of the man's words were garbled as Cyrus zoned out. His ears were only tuned to the phrase which would allow him to leave his position to claim his woman. The second the words left the Reverend's lips, Cyrus nearly leapt from the dais, clasping Atarah's hand in his.

The slight tremble in her fingers caught him unawares. Giving them a reassuring squeeze, he stared into her eyes, searching them for any signs of distress. Hers didn't hold the sheen of unshed tears, nor a hint of uncertainty at what they were doing. The only indicator she wasn't completely calm and in control was that slight tremor.

Uncaring about how it looked or what Reverend Hall had moved on to the next portion of the service, Cyrus leaned over. Speaking directly into her ear, he reassured her.

"Everything will be okay." When he pulled back, a barely perceptible nod was her only acknowledgement of his words.

Once he faced forward, he discovered Reverend Hall had stopped speaking and was staring at him expectantly.

"Can we continue now?"

The jokingly sarcastic lilt to his question sent tinkling sounds of laughter through the assembled guests. Cyrus didn't care. So long as Atarah was okay, they could laugh at him all they wanted. The increase in pressure on his fingers brought his gaze back to hers.

Her smile smoothed the frown dipping his brow when the pastor questioned him. Returning it, he rubbed his thumb along the back of her hand, gave her a wink, then looked back to the cheeky reverend. The man was slightly shorter than him, however the elevation of the dais put them at nearly the same height. With a single raised eyebrow and a small shake of the head, Reverend Hall continued with the ceremony.

While Cyrus listened intently as the pastor extolled the virtues of marriage and how it was smiled upon, he was anxious. He'd hidden it well, but the glimmer of anxiety he'd felt in Atarah's trembling digits had trickled into him. She hadn't said no when Reverend Hall had asked if she'd take Cyrus in marriage, but they hadn't made it to the exchange of rings nor the recitation of vows. She could still back out.

Even if he was certain, if she fled he'd follow her then convince her to come back. No matter how slight, there was the possibility she could still call the whole thing off.

The loosening of his muscles, releasing the tension in his shoulders and back didn't occur until she'd held out her left hand, with steady fingers, for him to slide the rings on. The platinum, diamond inlaid wedding band perfectly complimented the engagement ring making up the bridal set. The rings themselves only mattered to him, because she'd actually allowed him to put them on her finger.

She'd stared into his eyes as he'd repeated the words from the pastor. The light sheen of tears in her eyes didn't appear the least sorrowful. To top it off, when she took his hand to place the matching band on his finger, her voice was clear as she spoke the words binding them together for the rest of their lives.

"I, Atarah Grace Cox, take you, Cyrus Joseph Lauder, to be my lawfully wedded husband."

The rest of what she said was drowned out by the sound of his blood rushing so loudly, he couldn't hear anything else. That was until Reverend Hall said those magic words.

"Now, by the power vested in me, I pronounce you husband and wife. You may kiss your bride."

Cyrus needed little encouragement. Thankful for Atarah's height keeping him from having to pick her up, he captured her lips in a kiss which was decidedly a promise of what was to come. The polite clapping turned to cheering, prompting him to finally release her.

Running his tongue over his lips to claim all of her taste, Cyrus was proud of the dazed expression she wore. On autopilot, he turned, tucking her hand into the curve of his elbow, when the pastor's voice boomed out.

"I now present to you, Mr. and Mrs. Cyrus Joseph Lauder."

Cyrus's smile was wide as he escorted his wife back down the aisle and through the double doors. They still had to take their couple's pictures. First, Rita had instructed them to go straight to the staging room until she could get the guests moved to the out of the way reception area. Leading Atarah into the space, he was acutely aware of everything about her.

Naturally stunning, she emitted an ethereal glow beyond her normal beauty. The bountiful curves that constantly tempted him were encased in a white satin and lace dress with a fitted bodice, lifting her breasts up like a sumptuous offering. The lower half of the dress was also sculpted to her body, then flared slightly, beginning about mid-thigh. The train wasn't overly long, but he bent to pick it up to keep it from being trapped by the door before closing it behind them.

"Thank you."

"You're welcome."

Her voice was soft. Just above a whisper. Almost as if she didn't want to break the spell by speaking too loudly. Cyrus could understand. The past four months had been nothing short of interesting and had been peppered with more than a few of their trademark arguments. He figured they were on the same page, with neither of them wanting that to happen today.

Stepping closer to her, he slid his arms around her the way he wanted to when he first saw her in her wedding dress. Hell, as he'd wanted to do too many times to count in the past. Now that they were married, he could admit, if only to himself, part of his animosity stemmed from having such a delectable treat dangled in his face while not being able to touch it—let alone taste it.

"What are you doing?" The sharpness in Atarah's voice made him pull back to look down into her face.

"Holding my wife." Cyrus didn't like the line which appeared between her eyebrows as she returned his stare.

## Chapter Four

"Why?" The single word was weighted with Atarah's confusion surrounding Cyrus's behavior.

From the moment the doors had opened, when she'd seen him standing between his brother and Reverend Hall, he hadn't been the man who'd spent the past two years as her adversary almost any time she suggested funneling monies into anything beyond their standard ministries. However, the man who stood beside her mentor looked like a man in love with the woman he was about to marry.

That couldn't be right. Cyrus tolerated her. Other than the heated kiss he'd planted on her in her office that fateful day, he hadn't hinted at wanting to do more—be more—than who they were.

Yet now, he was wrapping his arms around her, surrounding her in his warmth, making her feel...things. Things which could addle her thinking. She didn't like it.

"Why am I holding my wife? Because I can. I also think I've waited long enough for the privilege."

Stiffening in his embrace, Atarah tipped her chin up. He wasn't insanely tall, but it felt like it when she had to tilt her head back to make eye contact. At five-foot-ten, it wasn't often she had to do so. However, Cyrus's six-foot five bulky frame made it necessary.

"Just because we're married doesn't mean you own me, Cyrus Lauder. I'm not property."

Squirming in his embrace, she wasn't able to detach herself from his grip.

"I never said you were property. And why it is a problem for me to hold my wife?"

"You keep saying that like I'm really your wife!"

The moment Cyrus opened his mouth to respond, the door swung open. Rita stepped inside, followed by Reverend Hall and the photographer. The smile on the wedding planner's face gave no indication she'd overheard any of their exchange.

"Okay, you two, let's get these photos with Reverend Hall signing the marriage certificate."

Cyrus's body went stiffer than a piece of petrified wood. His fingers dug into her sides, making her gasp at the increased pressure. Reflexively, she delivered soothing pats to his biceps until he released her.

They spent the next five minutes or so standing where they were placed as the photographer snapped photos. When they were done, Atarah surprised herself with her response to Reverend Hall's parting wishes of congratulations. She actually leaned into Cyrus when he slipped an arm around her waist.

*Don't read too much into it.* That's what she told herself to stop from melting against his hard body. Hard bodies were rumored to be uncomfortable to lay on, but Cyrus seemed to be busting that rumor wide open. It was so confusing. But, Atarah didn't have time to dwell on it. Pictures with Reverend Hall were followed by photos with the rest of their small wedding party.

Although they'd had limited interactions, she liked Cyrus's brother, Caleb. The irreverence with which he handled his older brother never failed to make her smile or giggle. Cyrus took himself way too seriously. Caleb appeared to be the exact opposite.

While it was easy to believe Cyrus was the CEO of Lauder Industries. Knowing Caleb was the CFO was a little harder to sell. Him keeping Iva laughing as the photographer moved them around, also took Atarah's mind away from the photos. The one's they wouldn't be taking. The ones with the parents. Neither of their parents had shown up.

Both sets had been invited. Both had chosen to stay away. The reason for her parents' absence was well known, but Cyrus had simply offered a crisp, 'We're estranged' as the answer to why his parents declined. Atarah didn't push. Their rejection was enough without her forcing him to speak on it before he was ready.

The photos were followed by the reception being held in a ballroom, spilling out onto the terrace on the opposite side of the estate home. The location offered a stunning view of the setting sun.

Atarah was once again surprised by how easy it was to lean into Cyrus's touch as they went around thanking their guests. The meal was delicious, although she'd only eaten a few bites of each course. The atmosphere was light. People appeared genuinely happy for them. There was still a relatively large crowd assembled when they dashed off to the stretch SUV set to take them to the airstrip.

A chartered flight was waiting to spirit them away for their honeymoon. She had no idea where they were going. It was the one wedding detail Cyrus wouldn't divulge, stating he wanted it to be a surprise. Atarah let his adamance slide, since he was footing the bill for everything while she seemed to be getting the majority of the benefits.

Falling asleep leaning against the window only to awaken with Cyrus's chest beneath her cheek and his arm wrapped around her, was a bit startling for Atarah. More so because she found herself snuggling into his embrace before she caught herself and sat up straight.

"Are we there?" The motion of the plane felt different. Not waiting for an answer, her gaze swiveled to the window to see distant lights instead of the blackness of the night sky.

"The landing was soft, but it appears it woke you up anyway." Cyrus provided the answer while keeping his arm wrapped around her shoulders.

"Oh." Self-consciously wiping her face, she hoped she hadn't drooled on him. Fluffing at her hair was an afterthought as the plane glided to a stop.

Since they'd arrived at night, at a private airstrip, where she could see a vehicle was waiting for them on the tarmac, Atarah still had no idea where they were.

"Do I get to know where we are now?"

Rubbing along her arm, Cyrus shook his head, still stubbornly refusing to give up the information.

"You'll find out when we get there—not a second sooner, Miss Nosey."

"I don't think wanting to know where on earth I'm planting my behind for the next two weeks is being nosey. What if something happens to you? I'll need to be able to tell people where I am."

Shooting her a wry grin, Cyrus chuckled. "Dramatic much? Why can't you just let me surprise you? Is it really so hard?"

His question brought up an answer that she managed to keep trapped inside her mouth. She didn't want to revisit the near argument they'd had immediately after the wedding. Although she was genuinely confused as to why he was treating this like a real marriage and a honeymoon they'd both been anticipating.

Atarah was saved once again by the flight attendant. As she went about her landing routine, she informed them it was okay to unbuckle their safety belts and leave their seats. Thankful she'd changed out of her wedding dress into a travel outfit at the estate, Atarah stood once Cyrus stepped out to give her space.

The ride from the airstrip to their destination was equally unrevealing as her brief glimpse out of the window. Wherever they were, it wasn't densely populated. However, it was definitely somewhere tropical. Her brain fog didn't allow her to look at the time then calculate the possible locations based on the length of their flight. That was too much math with a sleep fogged brain.

Only the warmth and humidity gave her a clue to the locale. But those things didn't help her narrow it down. All she could do was resolve to wait until Cyrus was ready to tell her or a literal sign appeared in her line of sight.

The sign never appeared, but Cyrus finally revealed their location when the vehicle turned off the narrow two-lane road onto an equally narrow one. In the distance, she could see the outline of a structure which wasn't a hotel. As they drew closer, the outdoor lighting highlighted the villa. Atarah's jaw dropped. The place was too beautiful for words.

Cyrus's warmth invaded her personal space when he leaned over. "Welcome to Turks and Caicos."

Forgetting how close he was, Atarah whipped her head around. The action put them nose to nose. The words on the tip of her tongue died. Clamping her lips shut, she turned back toward the view from her window, ignoring the thundering pulse that was definitely too low on her anatomy to be considered her heart.

Thankfully, the driver was there to open the door, so she didn't have to address the tension coiling inside the SUV. Cyrus's hand closed over hers bathing it in the heat from his palm. Despite the tropical environment, Atarah didn't try to shake off his hold.

Staring at the two story, pristinely white house, Atarah shook her head. "I can't believe you brought us here."

"Why? Shouldn't we go somewhere nice for our honeymoon? Get away from the noise of the city? Relax and just enjoy one another?"

*Who was this man, and what had he done with Cyrus Lauder?* Atarah stared at the Cyrus doppelgänger, but offered nothing to refute what he'd said. Regardless of how out of character it seemed, it wasn't a lie. It had been far too long since her last peaceful getaway.

Cyrus tugged on her hand. "Come on. Let's go inside."

# Chapter Five

Atarah didn't have to tell Cyrus he'd shocked her. The wonder pooling in her eyes said it for her. On their best days, they were cordial and a bit stiff toward each other. But, since they announced their engagement, he'd been attempting to show her more of himself. Although, he was aware she thought it was a part of the ruse to make the membership believe they'd been secretly seeing one another for some time.

He didn't correct her, because he knew she was in for even more shocks to her system before it was all said and done. Guiding her up the stairs, they were met on the wide porch by an elderly couple. Their smiles were wide, giving off genuine warmth.

"Good evening, Mr. and Mrs. Lauder." With a slight Haitian lilt to her speech, the woman greeted them.

"I am Geneviève. This is my husband Francois."

"Nice to meet you." Cyrus's return greeting matched Atarah's.

Geneviève quickly went into her welcome speech giving them information about the house as she led them through the rooms. The last stop on the tour was the main suite where they'd sleep during their stay.

"Francois and I live on the property in a cottage that is close enough for us to get to you quickly if needed, but far enough way to afford you privacy."

Cyrus had to avert his gaze to keep from laughing at the scandalized expression on Atarah's face when Geneviève winked at her after she mentioned privacy. He wasn't bothered by the comment. They were newlyweds. Of course, they'd be expected to want privacy.

"If the two of you don't need anything, we are going to retire for the night. I've prepared light snacks and placed them in the refrigerator. I'll also see that your luggage is brought in on my way out."

Walking with Geneviève toward the front door, Cyrus thanked her for waiting up for them and keeping the house prepared. He was aware of Atarah following slowly behind them, but didn't attempt to force her to join the conversation. By the time they made it to the door, she was back at his side.

"Okay then. I see the young fellas have brought your belongings inside. So that is all for me tonight. You two have a lovely evening." Geneviève smiled as she accepted her husband's arm.

"Ring when you're ready for your first meal of the day."

Tossing Atarah another wink, the older woman squeezed her husband's arm. Once they reached the bottom of the stairs, Cyrus closed the door.

"Can you believe that woman? I mean, for the most part she was very pleasant. But what was with the winking? What does she think we're going to be doing over here?"

Atarah walked toward their luggage, looking over it like she was checking it for damage. Folding his arms across his chest, Cyrus leaned against the closed door.

"I'm pretty sure she thinks we're going to be fucking like bunnies all over this house."

"Cyrus!!" Atarah bolted upright and had the audacity to look at him as if he'd said something completely insane.

"What? We're newlyweds. That's what normally happens the first night, the second night. And if the guy's lucky, every night of the honeymoon."

Atarah looked over her shoulders as if to check to make certain no one was behind her, then looked back at Cyrus. Even the deep brown of her skin couldn't hide the flush creeping into her cheeks.

"Is that what you think we're going to be doing for the next two weeks? You think I'm going to let you—"

"Let me?" Cyrus was off the door and in her face before Atarah could finish the sentence. "Are you saying I'd force you to have sex with *your husband*? That if it happened, I'd somehow be taking advantage of you?"

If it were possible, steam would be coming from his nostrils with each exhale. And, while he was admittedly heated at her inference, their proximity...knowing they were alone for the foreseeable future, had him swelling in his pants with barely checked desire.

"Don't twist my words, Cyrus. I'm just saying." Atarah's sentence trailed off. She put her hand on the handle of her suitcase before taking a step back.

Before the wheeled luggage could move an inch, Cyrus replaced her hand with his, shuttling the rolling bag to the side. One step ate up ninety percent of the distance separating them.

"I'm not twisting your words and you didn't answer my question." Curling his fingers around her nape, he tangled them in the loose hair there. "Are you implying that fucking your husband will only happen at my insistence or by force?"

He couldn't stop himself from tracking the way her lips twisted and her eyebrow arched when she glared up at him.

"Of course not. I've had many thoughts about you, but I've never considered you a man who'd force a woman to have sex with him."

One corner of Cyrus's lips tipped up at her attempt to partially answer the question by focusing on the part he was certain she found most egregious.

"What about the rest, Pastor?"

Atarah's frown deepened. If he didn't know better, he would think she was genuinely confused. But he did. His wife was sharp. Her failure to address the entire statement wasn't done in error.

"Don't play with me, woman. You know how I feel about repeating myself."

"And I told you, that you aren't the boss of me, Cyrus Lauder."

At her heated declaration, Cyrus erased the remaining ten percent of space separating them.

"Oh yeah?" His voice sounded nearly feral to his own ears. "Let me show you something."

The words had narrowly hit the air before his mouth captured hers. Accepting the offering presented by her parted lips, he delved his tongue inside to tangle with hers. Her moan gave him oxygen as she melted against him. Her voluptuous curves felt amazing pressed to his chest and beneath his fingertips.

Skating his touch down her side, he reached around to tug her lower half closer to him. Her sharp inhale let him know she'd felt his hardness trying to escape the confines of his casual pants. Releasing her as abruptly as he'd begun the kiss, he stared into her face.

"Now, tell me you're not wet enough to fill a cup with your juices right now. Tell me that if I put my fingers inside you, they wouldn't come out completely coated in the evidence of how much you want me to fuck you."

Atarah's naturally long lashes lowered, covering her dark eyes —hiding them from him. Her bottom lip disappeared between her teeth, causing two dimples to appear next to her chin.

"What? Nothing to say?"

Her heaving breaths and avoidance of his gaze were clear answers, but Cyrus wasn't satisfied. He wanted the words— complete acknowledgement of her yearning for him.

"Come now, Pastor. Don't tell me you're suddenly shy. Not the woman who quotes lyrics to popular rap songs in her sermons. Where's the woman who stands up to me? The one who calls me a jackass to my face? Is she too afraid to admit she also wants me?

Too timid to say she wants me inside her so deep it's hard to tell where I stop and she begins? Or, that some of those thoughts she's had about me have been filthy, nasty things she doesn't want me to know about? Hmm?"

As he challenged her, Cyrus ghosted his fingers down the side of her neck then across the slight patch of exposed skin above the vee in the collar of her blouse. Keeping his gaze trained on her face, he felt the thumping of her pulse at the base of her neck. He had her. He knew it. She knew it. The only question was, how long would it take her to admit it.

Once she lifted her eyelids and stopped hiding from him, she also released her lip. Glistening with wetness, it tempted him to taste her again. He lowered his head, but held firm. The next move was hers.

"What's the matter, Pastor. Cat got your tongue?"

Instead of using the words swirling in her eyes, Atarah grabbed him by the front of his shirt. Using her hold as leverage, she tugged him closer while simultaneously lifting up on her toes. When her lips touched his, he didn't hold back the groan it elicited, but he didn't completely fold. Reluctantly tearing away, he pierced her with a determined look.

"Words, Atarah Lauder. Give them to me."

Fire blazed in her chocolate depths. Just when he thought she'd continue with her stubborn campaign, a breathy conciliation passed through her plush lips.

"Yes. Yes, I'm wet. Yes I want to fuck my husband." Her voice grew stronger with each word. By the time the last word floated between them, he was already lifting her into his arms and striding toward their bedroom.

# Chapter Six

Atarah turned off the part of herself which was screaming at her not to be foolish. Not to let Cyrus Lauder goad her into doing something she might regret later. Long before she'd committed herself to the ministry, she'd been called a prude by some, because she didn't believe in casual sex.

She didn't judge others for how they lived. But for her, sex didn't happen without feelings. If there weren't feelings beforehand, sex normally inspired them. As far as her lady bits were concerned, her heart was inextricably tied to it. Where one went, the other was sure to follow. Where would that get her in this fake marriage with Cyrus?

His body was hard beneath her fingertips as he carried her through their temporary home into the bedroom suite Geneviève had shown them just minutes before. As if her internal thoughts were written on her face, Cyrus's harsh glare bathed her upturned face.

"What's going on in that head of yours, Pastor? Did you actually think this was going to be a marriage in name only? That you'd get to sashay your beautiful ass in my face, and I'd never want to touch you?"

For a second, Atarah forgot how to inhale and exhale. Feelings of exposure had her wanting to shrink inside herself. But there was nowhere she could go to escape her new husband. He was already proving she couldn't hide from him—not even in her thoughts.

After he placed her on her feet beside the bed, his nimble fingers got to work on the ties holding her blouse together, relieving her of the garment in seconds. Goose pimples rose along her arms as the cool air wafted over her skin. They didn't stay long before the heat of Cyrus's touch banished them.

Dispensing kisses as he went along, he stripped her bare before guiding her onto the bed. The scrape of his beard as he placed his lips in various places was far more erotic than she'd imagined in her wildest fantasies. When his touch disappeared, Atarah couldn't prevent the moan of protest nor the pout which followed.

She tracked his movements as he stood from the bed and began shedding his clothes. The polo style shirt hit the floor, closely followed by the light brown slacks. When he lowered his boxer briefs, Atarah nearly swallowed her tongue. A battle ensued between her mouth and pulsing channel over which of them needed the moisture more.

Broad shoulders with a barrel chest tapered down to a trimmer waist. It wasn't a perfect vee, because he'd been gifted with a thick body. But *he* was perfect. The star of the perfection was the length jutting proudly out in front of him.

Cyrus's shaft was standing out from his pelvis flanked by long legs giving testament to his commitment to leg day. A shiny drop of moisture appeared at the tip of his manhood making her run her tongue over her bottom lip. The awe-filled words tumbled from her mouth without thought, but she couldn't snatch them back.

"Look at the blessings."

A cocky grin stretched across Cyrus's face. Tilting his head to one side as he stepped closer. He backed her farther onto the bed as he climbed over her.

"You think this is good? Let me show you something."

While his lips recaptured hers and their tongues dueled for dominance, his hands were busy acquainting themselves with her pleasure points. It felt like he had been given implicit instructions on what to do to please her, as he tweaked her nipples, showering them in kisses, and nibbles before sucking them into his mouth.

"Mmm!!" The moan ripped from Atarah's throat as he bit down on his captive sending a jolt of indescribable pleasure coursing through her.

"Mhm… You like that, huh? How about this?"

In a move which swiftly had him relocating to the space between her thighs, he tossed her legs onto his shoulders like they weren't as heavy as their thickness proclaimed. Her core clenched simply from the heat of his breath wafting over her lower lips. She had half a second to process before he delivered an open-mouthed kiss to her mons.

His groans vibrated against her sensitive folds taking her to the brink of orgasm in an embarrassingly short amount of time. Her fingers obeyed her unspoken command as they gripped his hair, holding his head as he delved his tongue inside her walls before flicking her clit, coaxing it out to play.

The sounds of pleasure Cyrus released as he devoured her, added to her own enjoyment. Her hips danced to an ancient tune, rocking and tilting. Growling something which sounded like a threat if she kept running from him, he wrapped his arms around her thighs locking her into position.

*Had she been running?* Atarah didn't think she had—even if the sensations capturing her focus made her simultaneously feel like climbing the wall to get away while rolling around in them to have them all over her body. The latter won out when Cyrus sucked her clit between his lips, using his tongue to torture the little bundle of nerves. Once his thick finger slipped into her channel and began to beckon her orgasm forward, she leapt over the cliff into oblivion.

"Aaah!! Shit!!"

"That's it. Give it to me."

Cyrus encouraged her from his position with his face planted in her pussy. Her body trembled as she tried to come down, but he remained in position lapping up his reward, grumbling his appreciation into her folds.

Just as the quivering was dying down, he rose on his haunches, taking her with him. The new position had her ankles near his ears and her ass being cupped in his hands. Looking down her body, Atarah watched him as he watched her. His gaze was glued to her still pulsing sex. While he licked his lips like he was contemplating going back in, her center clenched with anticipation.

"Later." The whispered promise was directed at her love box —not to Atarah. To her, he made a different promise.

"It's time to consummate our marriage, wife."

The word consummate had never been sexy when she'd heard it before. However, in Cyrus's baritone while his fingers gripped her ass and his thickness glided between her folds, it added to one of the most erotic statements to Atarah's ears. It was also her only warning.

The mushroom capped tip of Cyrus's length split her folds. And, for a second, it felt like it would split her in two as he fed the entirety of it into her slick channel. Her back left the soft sheets in a deep arch, and her fingers gripped them in tight fists.

She didn't care if she ripped the linens completely off of the bed. Atarah needed an anchor to withstand the sensual onslaught Cyrus's invasion rained down on her. The stretching of her walls as he steadily thrusted was amazing, with a tinge of pain. Just enough of both to have her natural juices bathing his turgid length as her husband sought to make good on his claim to fuck her until she didn't know where he ended and she began.

Rocking onto the crown of her head, Atarah's hips jerked in his hold. Her channel clenched around his tunneling thickness, drawing a strangled curse from Cyrus's lips. There was no doubt her posterior would bear the imprint of his long digits from the tightness of his grip. His sounds of appreciation mingled with hers.

"What do you think you're doing?"

The harsh timbre of Cyrus's voice prompted Atarah to attempt to open her eyes because her tongue wasn't cooperating with her vocal cords to produce coherent words. The fierceness of his expression caused her walls to clamp tighter around his questing shaft.

Muttering about it being her fault, Cyrus pressed her knees toward her armpits then began a deliciously punishing campaign to drive Atarah insane. At least that's how it felt. The sensations were so all-consuming she couldn't do anything but accept the beautifully brutal way he invaded her core, stimulating the special place inside her.

It wasn't long after the imaginary switch flipped that she was flung into another orgasm. This time, Cyrus joined her. With his hips jerking erratically, grinding his pelvic bone against her overstimulated clit, he bathed her insides with his essence.

Their appreciative exclamations joined together to create an erotic soundtrack, bouncing off the walls as they reveled in their first lovemaking session as husband and wife.

Cyrus lowered her legs, but didn't separate from her quivering core. Instead, he braced himself above her on his elbows, raining feathery kisses on her face before ending with gentle pecks to her lips. Atarah's eyes lowered to half mast, heavy in the aftermath of their activities.

"Mmm... Now that we have round one out of the way. We can take our time and really explore."

Atarah's eyelids snapped open. "I'm sorry. What?"

# Chapter Seven

Sunlight warmed Cyrus's shoulder as it cascaded over the bed hitting him across his upper back. He was lying on his side, with his head propped on his fist, watching Atarah sleep. Her breathing was even, and she looked so content in her slumber. Which was a feat, after the ways he'd worked her body the previous night.

At one point, even to him, it felt like he was attempting to crawl inside her skin. He couldn't get enough of his wife. Now that he had explicit permission to touch and taste every part of her, he didn't think he'd be able to stop himself. There was the slightest hitch in Atarah's breathing, then it changed.

"It's creepy to watch someone while they're sleeping."

Atarah mumbled her complaint without opening her eyes. Not responding, Cyrus simply marveled at the seamlessness of her waking process. There wasn't a jerk, nor squinting eyes, rubbing or even a stretch. She just came to wakefulness with full awareness of her surroundings. When she finally opened her eyes, she peered up at him for a moment before rolling to her side, facing away from him.

The hand he'd rested on her hip slid across her lower back as she rearranged herself. It would've fallen when she sat up if he hadn't adjusted himself, tightening his hold. Glancing over her shoulder, Atarah gripped his fingers.

"Relax, Cerberus. I'm just going to the bathroom."

"If I'm Cerberus, does that make you the underworld?"

Making a teeth sucking sound, she swatted at his hands until he released her. Cyrus caught the grin she tried to hide, and it broadened the smile on his face. He was positive he'd been smiling wider than a circus clown in the twenty or so hours which had passed since she'd officially become his wife.

Hearing the sound of running water, he left the bed. With a perfunctory knock, he pushed the door open. Atarah's glare could've burned him to cinders and her words might've done the job if she didn't have a toothbrush in her mouth. Ignoring her irritation, Cyrus tapped her ass as he passed her, entering the water closet.

Continuing his irreverent campaign, he stood before the toilet relieving himself without bothering to close the door. Choking noises made him poke his head back around the door frame.

"Are you okay?"

Wiping her mouth, Atarah met his gaze in the mirror.

"Am I okay? You just barged in on me, not wearing a stitch of clothing, then waltzed into the toilet where you started urinating without so much as closing the door."

Finished with his task, Cyrus flushed the toilet and joined her at the sink. Flicking on the hot water, he pumped liquid soap into his hands.

"So...I take that as a no."

"You think?"

Atarah folded her arms beneath her breasts, unwittingly drawing his attention to her impressive cleavage peeking through the vee at the neck of her robe. A robe he considered completely unnecessary attire. Standing before her wearing nothing, Cyrus matched her pose.

"What's the problem? We're married. We'll be sharing space. I *did* knock before I came in."

"You knocked and didn't wait for an answer. I could've been naked."

Gesturing to his state of undress, Cyrus stared at her. "You say that like I haven't seen you naked or didn't just spend a large chunk of last night putting my hands and other parts all over and *in* you."

The way she wrinkled her nose at him would've been cute if she wasn't in the process of being delusional and giving him shit.

"Must you be so crass?"

Stepping into her space, Cyrus tugged her arms free to allow him to pull her body flush with his.

"Must you be so... Whatever this is you're pretending to be."

"I'm not pretending I don't want you walking into the bathroom I'm occupying without an invitation."

Raising a single eyebrow, Cyrus pierced her with a direct stare. "Are you telling me you expect us to behave as strangers, rather than who we are to each other?"

"Being my husband doesn't give you the right to invade my private time."

Vaguely, Cyrus heard the words she spoke after she said 'husband', but his comprehension skills dropped significantly when his cock plumped upon hearing her say the title. Until this moment, she'd used the word sparingly. Once during the actual wedding ceremony then again, when he'd forced her to acknowledge she desired him as much as he desired her.

A fog of lust descended on him. Cyrus went with it. He didn't want to argue. He wanted to fuck his wife. Have her scream his name and her voice give out from her many exclamations of pleasure. It was already slightly scratchy, but he was certain he could do better.

"Cyrus, what are you doing?"

Not immediately responding, he continued with his new quest, loosening the tie on the silk robe. The second the knot gave way, Cyrus was pushing it from her shoulders.

"I would think it's obvious. Maybe you'll see things more clearly when we get rid of this thing."

Grabbing at the edges of the robe, Atarah tried and failed to look scandalized.

"Seriously, Cyrus you can't want to do...*that*... again right now."

"Why can't I?" Pausing, his hands rested on her bare hips with his fingertips grazing the sides of her tempting ass. He searched her face.

"Are you too sore?" As much as he wanted to sink inside her, he wouldn't purposely hurt her. There were other ways to derive pleasure, to soothe Atarah's ache.

"Is saying yes the only thing that would keep you from trying to use sex to avoid having a serious conversation?"

"No, but I'm done talking about us sharing space. We'll figure out what works for both of us in time. Now isn't the time for you to hide from me."

Tugging the edges of the robe from her fingers, he finished removing it, tossing it to the side. Cupping her breasts, he lifted the heavy globes, stroking his thumbs over her distended nipples.

"I...ummm... I'm not hiding."

"Mhmm..." Leaning down, he captured one turgid peak between his lips, worrying it with gentle nips before releasing it in a suckling pop. "So, what do you call it?"

"Umm..."

Moving to the other breast, Cyrus began giving it the same treatment.

"Tell me, Pastor. What do you call it when you leave your new husband in bed, cover your beautiful body, then make a fuss about him joining you?"

How he was still capable of making complete sentences was a mystery, because his length pulsed to enter her silken walls. He didn't have to look down at it to know it was jutting out in front of him like a battering ram. And battering was its primary goal. As if it had a mind separate from the brain housed between his ears, Cyrus's thickness strained with the desire to be joined with Atarah's heated core once again.

A whispered jumble of words tumbled from his wife's lips, but Cyrus's senses were too overwhelmed to decipher them. despite him having demanded an answer. To him, she might as well have pressed the trigger of a starting pistol, because the race was on. Although, this portion might be a sprint, it was destined to be a multi-leg event.

Turning her to allow her to lean against the vanity for support, he took her lips in a kiss telegraphing the promises he intended to keep. The minty flavor of her toothpaste lingered on her tongue as she moaned under his amorous attention. Releasing her mouth, Cyrus trailed kisses down her body, stopping briefly to pay homage to her succulent breasts, he continued until he was on his knees in front of her.

Encouraging her to rest fully against the vanity, he parted her legs. Running a finger down her slit, he licked his lips in anticipation. Referencing the question he'd asked about her hiding, he leaned closer to her honeyed haven.

"You don't want to tell me? That's okay. I'm sure Rapture will tell me all about it."

Slickness met the tip of his nose when he pressed it against the hood shielding her clit before he angled his head, delving his tongue between her folds. As he suspected, Rapture was already wet and eager for his attention. The offering was enough to send him seeking more as he devoured her sweetness. It was past breakfast time, but there was no need for him to ring anyone to bring nourishment. He had everything he required at the apex of his wife's thighs.

"Cyrus!" Atarah's cries hit the air as she held on to his head with one hand, her thighs locked in a campaign to make this spot his permanent home.

Her cries of release were encouragement to amplify his efforts. He didn't stop until her legs were shaking, and she was slumped back on the vanity with her shoulders resting on the mirror.

# Chapter Eight

The man was trying to kill her. Atarah was convinced Cyrus intended to deplete her of all bodily fluids via orgasm. The cool glass against her shoulders did very little to calm the flame he'd ignited when he'd planted his face between her thighs. Her devout upbringing didn't mean she'd come to the marriage bed pure.

So, Cyrus wasn't the first man she'd been with. He was however, the only one who displayed such enthusiasm and prowess in *all* areas of lovemaking. She was quickly learning that very little was off limits. Also, he was insatiable. Whether he was that way in general or only with her wasn't a question she wanted an answer to at the moment.

Honestly, Atarah didn't think her brain could handle any additional information, even if her ego wanted to know if she was his muse. Egos got people in trouble. It was best not to yield to that particular personality trait.

While she attempted to reacquaint herself with the process of exchanging oxygen and carbon dioxide, Cyrus was kissing her mons. Which, unless her ears were playing tricks on her, he'd nicknamed Rapture. If she had the extra energy, Atarah would roll her eyes at his unique turn of phrase.

Were she a betting woman, she would've wagered nothing could make the word pastor sound like anything other than what it was. A title used to refer to clergy. Not when Cyrus Lauder said it. Especially not when he said it while torturing her senses with sensual innuendo.

From partially lowered lids, Atarah watched him rise from between her spread legs. Calling his forty-two years a liar, he stood easily. The thickness jutting from between his hips immediately caught her eye. A pearlescent drop of pre-cum formed on the tip as she stared at it. Without thought, her tongue swiped across her bottom lip.

"Are you having carnal thoughts about me, Pastor?"

Denial was on the tip of Atarah's tongue until Cyrus swiped his thumb across the head of his shaft. Without a word, her mouth opened when he presented the digit to her. Sucking it into her mouth, she closed her eyes when his flavor hit her tongue. *This was so wrong...Or was it?* After all, what happens between a husband and wife is between them. Right?

A moan of protest pushed from her throat when Cyrus pulled his thumb away.

"Don't worry, baby. You'll get to have your fun. But first...Let me show you something."

Those five words were beginning to have a Pavlovian effect on Atarah. Her core clenched then a surge of adrenaline coursed through her body. Giving her a feral grin, Cyrus draped her legs over his arms, aimed his stiffness at her center, and slid home. As her channel stretched to accommodate him, she enjoyed the slight twinge of pain accompanying his invasion of her core.

Her hips didn't consult her when they began winding, lifting and lowering her to meet his firm thrusts. A sheen of sweat glistened on Cyrus's muscles giving Atarah the insane urge to lick him. All over. The thought was pushed to the side when he pulled out, tugged her from the countertop, bent her over then plunged back into her still grasping depths.

Sweet savior, this man was going to send her straight to Hades, and she would happily pack the bag for a taste of what he delivered. The blended sounds of their pleasure bounced off the surfaces of the bathroom combining with the slap-thwap noises generated by their skin meeting with each of Cyrus's forceful thrusts.

The smooth countertop offered Atarah nowhere to grip to hold on when their activities moved her around on the slab. Her nipples puckered in response to the contact with the cold vanity. However, it was no match for the heat radiating from her core and spreading throughout her body. Unexpected warmth covered one breast, separating it from the icy surface, when Cyrus cupped it. A tweaking twist to her nipple acted as a tuner for her sweet spot. Her walls clenched around his length in response to the attention her sensitive peak received.

"Fuck!" Curses fell from Cyrus's lips. Atarah was no longer able to form words to agree with him. Gasps, moans and incoherent babble were her language until further notice.

In a change he'd been priming her for, Cyrus angled his hips, hitting that special place inside her. Pleasure locked Atarah's limbs when he added clitoral stimulation to the equation. The pressure from the twisting pinch to her nipple catapulted her into a leg-shaking, back arching orgasm.

"Oh damn..." Cyrus's words met the air in a huff.

His measured strokes became jerky. She couldn't move if she wanted to, but he placed his large hands on her hips, holding her in place as his length pulsed inside her. Looking into the mirror, Atarah watched his face. An expression of pleasure-filled awe covered it while his eyes were glued to where they were joined. It was as if he was being held in a trance by the visual—very similar to how she felt observing him.

Unguarded, his features held...devotion? Closing her eyes to cut off the thought-provoking image, Atarah allowed the pleasurable after effects to roll through her from Cyrus reaching his peak.

The empty feeling from him removing his thickness from her channel prompted a sharp inhale. Soothing caresses to her bottom and back were delivered from her husband's lightly calloused digits. *How did a corporate guy get callouses?* The thought was in her head then gone just as quickly as it appeared, when he lifted her sated body in a bridal carry.

"Oh!" Grabbing onto his shoulders, Atarah's eyes flew to his face.

Grinning smugly, Cyrus offered no comment to her surprise at being lifted into his arms. She wasn't close to being a lightweight, but it didn't seem to matter to him. He didn't so much as grunt with the action. She didn't ask where they were going. There was no need.

Placing her on her feet in front of the glass shielding the shower, reminiscent of a spa, he slid the door open and reached inside. The patter of water hitting the tiled surface became the dominant sound in the space. They didn't speak. It was as if a spell had been woven around them, and neither of them wanted to risk breaking it.

Cleansing their bodies, they explored, but didn't fall into lustful coupling again. Assisting one another, they bathed. The intimacy of the moment didn't escape Atarah. Try as she might to wall off her feelings, she didn't think she succeeded.

In the short time since they'd officially become husband and wife, they hadn't been the people they'd shown one another for the past two years. At least, it was how it felt to her. In one sense, it wasn't simply that she didn't recognize Cyrus. To a degree, she didn't recognize herself.

It was ridiculously easy for her to fall into the carnal side of their union, despite her assertion it wasn't a real marriage. What did her quick acquiescence say about her? Especially when the man she'd wed had been the opposition all this time.

Once they'd dried off and he'd completed his morning routine, Cyrus left her in the bathroom. While she dealt with her hair, she wasn't sure what he was doing. Although the look he shot her when he exited, leaving the door wide open, let her know his thoughts on their previous conversation. Not wanting to argue, she let the non-verbal demand hang between them.

When she was done twisting her thick hair into something she could live with, she tossed on the first comfortable pieces of clothing she put her hand on from her luggage. Cyrus wasn't in the bedroom. Without thinking too deeply about it, Atarah wandered out in search of her husband.

# Chapter Nine

Sitting back in his chair, Cyrus observed Atarah seated across from him at the small bistro style table. They were having a late breakfast outside, overlooking the pristine beach. She'd been surprised to find him putting the meal together when she'd finished with her hair.

He was proud of himself for not making mention of his plans to mess up her carefully constructed hair style. Cyrus preferred when her locks held that just-fucked look as they had earlier. Although she'd complained about forgetting her hair bonnet, he'd been proud of occupying her to such a degree she hadn't the presence of mind to do more than drop off into dreamland.

Atarah had been in deep slumber when he'd cleaned them both up before wrapping his body around hers then drifting off to sleep himself. It had been one of the most restful nights he'd experienced in quite some time. Even when taking their vigorous activities into consideration, he'd felt completely refreshed when he woke with the sun.

The environment was so calm. Their breakfast was so peaceful; he didn't want to risk tampering with it. But he knew they needed to talk. They had to clear the air. It needed to be known and understood, no matter the circumstances surrounding their quick engagement and marriage, they *would* have a real marriage. In every sense of the word. He'd settle for nothing less.

With his gaze glued to her lush lips, he watched them purse, moving while she chewed the last bite of fruit from her plate. Not breaking his gaze, he finally spoke.

"We need to talk."

Atarah paused with the glass partway to her mouth. Apparently deciding to forgo the last sip of her juice, she placed it back onto the table.

"So, *now* you want to talk?"

"Careful, Pastor. Your smart mouth will get you fucked."

"Cyrus!"

He couldn't stop the lecherous grin from taking over his face. She actually put her hand to her neck, reaching for pearls to clutch. There weren't any there. But, it didn't stop her from reaching for them.

"Don't, Cyrus, me. I'm giving you fair warning. You're the one who can't seem to resist being snarky."

Atarah's jaw dropped. Cyrus watched as it snapped closed. Her thought process was painted across her face. He observed the exact moment she decided to try a different tactic.

"I'm not snarky. I simply made an observation. I've attempted to speak with you, and you've avoided it. Which begs the question. Are we only going to have genuine conversations on your terms?

Lifting one eyebrow, he silently regarded her for a few moments before responding. Choosing his words carefully, he leaned forward getting as close as the small table would allow without standing.

"It sounds an awful lot like you're saying I don't take your wants seriously. Which isn't true. And I don't want to argue. When I said we need to talk, I meant *talk*. Not trade barbs. It would be nice if we weren't constantly at odds."

Cyrus knew he'd earned every second of her silent, skeptical, consideration of his statement. Atarah's arms were folded across her breasts. He wasn't sure if it was a protective gesture, or if she was closing herself off to him. His first inclination was to press forward, but he fought against the urge.

The next move was hers to make. He was fine with laying his cards on the table. However, he didn't want to be out there exposed and alone. It was together or nothing. And, since nothing wasn't an option, he waited.

In slow increments, some of the tension left her shoulders. Then her arms loosened until her hands were resting in her lap. Her head tilted slightly to one side the way it did when she was considering something, yet hadn't quite made up her mind. Finally, she spoke.

"Okay. Sure. Let's really talk."

Relaxing against the back of his seat, he left his hands on the table. Splaying his fingers on the surface, he looked down at his digits then back up at his wife.

"Before, after the wedding, then again last night. You said something... I'm not sure how to take it, and I think we need to discuss it to be certain we're on the same page."

Her bottom lip disappeared for a moment before it reappeared, but she didn't speak. No snippy comeback. No filling in the gaps with what she thought he meant. Silence was her response to his assertion.

"I know the circumstances leading to us being in this situation. And, I know the common goal we both had for going to such an extreme. But, I don't think I'm wrong in saying you didn't expect us to have a real marriage. Since, you used those exact words yesterday.

I'm going with, that's what you thought. I just don't understand how you came to the conclusion we'd have a marriage in name only. Can you explain it to me?"

A prominent line appeared between Atarah's eyebrows and her nose scrunched slightly. The way she stared at him briefly made him think she didn't intend to answer.

"Can you explain to me why you *do* want a real marriage with me? Almost from the moment I accepted the position as senior pastor at Harmony Haven, we've been at odds. It felt like you'd say something which was clearly yellow was pink, simply to be on the opposing side of what I said.

You've never liked me. At best, we've managed to be civil to one another during that time. For me, I tried not to take offense to your opposition. Because, when it came down to it, it seemed like, you genuinely thought you were acting in the best interest of the church. Which is something I can respect —even if we disagree. But, you have to admit, most of our interactions were in some way contentious. What about our situation would lead me to believe this could be more than simply a means to an end?"

Gently tapping the table top, Cyrus gathered his thoughts. While she made valid points, her perceptions of him skewed reality. However, pointing it out to her would entail a delicate process. Otherwise, they'd be right back to the snark and barbs. Then, he'd end up using sex to shut her up. It wouldn't be a physical sacrifice. It also wouldn't help them move their relationship forward in a healthy manner.

"You're right. We haven't had many conversations which didn't devolve into strain, tension, or an argument. But, you're wrong about something. I *never* disliked you. ***Ever***."

Staring at her, he let the quietness hang between them for a moment while his statement set in. It seemed he'd shocked his feisty little pastor into silence. Her lack of immediate rebuttal made him wonder how she'd perceived their interactions.

"Forgive me if I'm having trouble correlating what you said with your actions in the past. It always seemed like I had to prove things to you for you to get on board with any suggestion I made."

"That's not entirely true." Cyrus uttered the counter state-ment in a soft tone. He couldn't allow her to continue to paint the narrative of him constantly contradicting her.

Her eyebrows shot up, and she adjusted her posture. She didn't fully return to her folded arm stance, but he noted a definite stiffening in her carriage.

"It's not true?"

"No. It's not. If you're really honest with yourself, you know it's not. There were numerous times when I was in agreement with you."

"Like when?" Having tossed it back to him for an example, she folded her arms again. This time, it was in the classic posture of a person who knew they were right.

"I was completely on board with you when you suggested the church turn the previous pastoral residence into a rental property. It made sense. You'd already purchased a home in the Logan City area and had no need of the residence. The property would've been empty when it could be used to generate revenue."

One eyebrow quirked, but she remained silent. It was enough for him to know she couldn't refute him. The bonus was knowing she was likely going through her memories cataloguing more than a few such moments.

# Chapter Ten

Ugh! Internally, Atarah rolled her eyes. On the outside, she simply stared at the man she'd married. Cyrus was right. He hadn't fought her on *everything*. It simply felt that way. Likely because of the moments he'd chosen to dig his heels in.

She didn't like how it made her feel when he openly contradicted her in front of the rest of the board, forcing her to prove her point before he'd yield. Not one to weaponize the pulpit to get her way, as she'd known her father to do on more than one occasion, she had to resort to using the church bylaws to remind him of the reach of her authority as the CEO of Harmony Haven.

However, she had stooped to that level. Once. Just once. And it had landed her in a chair on a balcony overlooking the ocean with a sore vajayjay aching for more of the thing which caused the soreness to begin with. Eventually, he'd conceded her point about the Lloyd property. Until now, she'd convinced herself he'd done so out of the pretense of selling them being a couple while removing himself from being contentious with her in front of others.

But now... Allowing her internal eyeroll to peek out, she dropped her folded arms. Resting her hands in her lap again, she shot him a glance.

"Fine. Maybe you don't contradict me on *everything*. But, we seem to have a fundamental difference of opinion when it comes to our roles and responsibilities."

Running a hand over his beard, Cyrus's nod was barely noticeable. Atarah *did* notice it, though. Standing, he began stacking their empty plates, gathering them in one hand.

"That's a longer discussion. Why don't we take this conversation inside, or move to a place with more comfortable seating?"

With their empty glasses in one hand and the half full pitcher of orange juice in the other, Atarah followed him inside. As they worked together to clean the kitchen, Cyrus was the first to re-initiate the conversation.

Although she clearly remembered Geneviève telling them they didn't have to worry about cooking and cleaning for themselves, Atarah simply toiled alongside her husband as they began the process of truly getting to know one another. She hoped that by the end of their talk, she'd understand why he was so adamant about their marriage being more than simply for show.

"I was raised in the church. Not one like Harmony Haven, but still a *Christian* church with my father being the only minister for many years."

Drying the plate in her hand, Atarah simply nodded, listening. She recalled him mentioning his father's profession, and she remembered seeing the title of Reverend on the wedding invitation they sent to his parents. The way he said the word

*Christian* projected all of his scorn at whatever he'd experienced growing up. As the child of a minister, and being one herself, she understood certain things could cause a person to become jaded in regard to those proclaiming to be members of the faith.

She listened silently as he talked about how his father often yielded to the dictates of their church board in order to stay in their good graces, as well as those of the bishops. Until he'd mentioned the name of the church, she wasn't aware he'd been raised in a fundamentalist offshoot of the Evangelical church.

His recounting of his father's experiences with the leadership of the Covenant of Faith Assembly gave her more clarity. Cyrus was accustomed to the board telling the pastor how things would go then the party line being towed without question. Her upbringing, while in some ways mirrored his, gave her a different perspective on the relationship between the minister and the church leadership.

Atarah's father, the Right Reverend Luther Cox, didn't play that. Staunchly old school, Forest Hill Baptist church was *his* church. The very idea of having anyone's word or authority exceed his was unimaginable. She had no doubt, at least a small part of his mindset played a role in how she dealt with the church board.

However, unlike her father, she could accept dissenting opinions. When they made sense. Also, Harmony Haven was a non-denominational church. So, they didn't strictly hold to the structure of other churches. The Head Pastor was also the CEO of their organization. Which came with its own set of responsibilities.

The more Cyrus spoke, she was forced to face one of the primary reasons for their issues communicating, in regard to the church. While their experiences as preacher's kids had similarities, the lessons their fathers unknowingly taught them were different.

When Cyrus trailed off, with seemingly nothing else to add, Atarah picked up the conversational thread. She was mildly surprised with how easily she was able to share with him.

"I guess it's true what they say. People can live almost identical lives and still come away from it having learned different things."

Warmth permeated the thin layer of material separating his hand from her leg as he rubbed her thigh. Not sexually. In a way which conveyed his support of her picking at the scab of her emotional wound.

"My father was...*is* an old school Baptist preacher. When I say old school, I mean pre-civil rights old school. Nothing happened at our church without his stamp of approval. No money was spent, no program was implemented, and the doors didn't open unless he'd put his key in the lock then pushed them open himself.

I never wanted to be exactly like him, but in some ways, I saw the benefit of having decisive leadership. Without it, people could stay locked in discussions. What-ifs and what-about-isms would rule until nothing got done. So, I've tried to take the good parts of what I learned from all of those years watching him."

"Is having a father who totally controlled everything the reason you don't like to listen?"

Shooting him a severe side eye glance, Atarah bit back her knee jerk response. *Mostly*.

"I thought we weren't going to argue?"

Cyrus had the audacity to look sincerely confused by her assessment. "I'm not arguing. I asked a question."

Lifting a single eyebrow, she tilted her head back. "You asked a question encased in an accusation."

After a few beats, understanding finally replaced his confused expression. "I apologize."

"Mm-hm." Atarah didn't dig into whether his apology was genuine.

"Let me rephrase." Squeezing her leg, he rubbed the outside of her thigh with his thumb. His mouth opened and closed a few times, yet he never actually composed a sentence.

"You can't figure out how to say it without being offensive can you?"

A wry grin accompanied the glance he shot in her direction. "I'm trying here."

Placing her hand on his, she wrapped her fingers around his hand, but didn't link them with his.

"I can tell. Anyway, I *do* listen. I just happen to have my own opinion and don't lack the vocabulary to express myself."

Cyrus turned his hand over, doing what she hadn't, tangling their fingers together.

"Does expressing your opinion always have to be contrary to mine?"

"When you aren't seeing the big picture? Yes."

"How am I missing it?"

The honesty of his words and facial expression allowed Atarah to truly feel as if it was safe to express her perspective without it devolving into a contentious situation. So, for the first time, they were able to really air things out. They talked for what seemed like forever, easily flowing from one topic to another.

They only stopped because of a knock on the door. Noticing the time, they realized it was mid-afternoon. They'd been talking for hours. Cyrus opened the door. From her position on the sofa, Atarah saw Geneviève's generous frame at the same time she heard her voice.

"I didn't want to be a bother, but you didn't ring and the day is almost gone."

Stepping inside when Cyrus moved, she wore a smile which widened when she made eye contact with Atarah sitting on the sofa. With her positioned directly in the middle, it was obvious the two had been close together before the interruption.

Waving her into the room, Cyrus spoke for the two of them. "It's no bother, Mrs. Laguerre. We--"

"Psh! Call me Geneviève."

Nodding in deference, Cyrus continued, "we used the items you stocked for us to prepare a late breakfast."

"Breakfast?" Geneviève sounded affronted. "Breakfast time was more than five hours ago! It's done two-thirty, almost three. What about your midday meal?"

As if the simple mention of food was all it took, Atarah's stomach grumbled. Although it wasn't loud enough for the others to hear, the protest from Cyrus's empty belly took care of the notifications.

"See!" Geneviève flipped her hand toward Cyrus's stomach. "I can see the two of you left on your own will waste away to bones."

Shaking her head, she made a beeline to the kitchen. "Don't worry. I thought ahead. I have something quick to put a lump in your bellies."

With her declaration, she left them both staring in her wake. Looking from the empty doorway to each other, they barely suppressed their laughter.

"Sister Monty." They both said the name together before covering their mouths to smother giggles.

Something had seemed familiar about Geneviève when they'd met, but Atarah couldn't put her finger on it. However, when she began fussing at them about forgetting to eat, it clicked. She reminded Atarah of one of their elderly church members. The woman made the best cream cheese pound cake on this side of heaven.

Of course, thinking of Sister Monty took her mind to the last time they'd served dinner at the church. She'd been unable to get away in time to actually sit for the meal with the congregation. Atarah's laughter dried up and she gave her husband the stink eye.

Looking as guilty as he was, Cyrus threw up his hands. "How many times do I have to say I'm sorry? I didn't know they'd set that piece of cake aside for you. It was right next to the plate Sister Mary pointed out to me when I went to pick up my food."

# Chapter Eleven

Atarah left him in the living room to follow Geneviève into the kitchen. Their voices filtered back to him as his wife engaged the older woman in a conversation about the island and possible activities for them to do away from the villa.

Cyrus was well aware he'd managed to skate by answering Atarah's primary question regarding why he wanted to marry her. Their conversation had covered a variety of topics while managing to shine a light on why they appeared to be at odds with one another so often. But, he hadn't given her a direct answer to her question as to why he wanted a real marriage with her.

She'd been pretty clear about why she didn't expect them to behave as a traditional married couple, still he had barely dipped a toe into his reasoning for wanting her to be his wife in every way. Doing so would expose far more than telling her about his life as the eldest son of Abraham Lauder. The father who acquiesced to every whim of their church council, but ran their home with an iron fist.

Having shed the wealth he'd been born into, Cyrus's father tried to live out many scriptures literally. Which meant estrangement from his own father, who he referred to as a philanderer. The only interaction Cyrus and Caleb were allowed with their grandparents was mainly due to their grandmother. And, the only gift they could accept was their grandfather paying for the both of them to attend the Little Shepherd's Summer Camp in Michigan.

It wasn't exactly where his grandparents wanted them to go each summer, but they conceded because it was the place their father considered safe from the worldly corruption Cornelius Lauder might expose them to. In an unspoken agreement, neither Cyrus, Caleb nor their grandparents mentioned that they'd purchased a home near the camp. It was how they were able to spend weekends with their grandparents unbeknownst to their parents.

"Okay. I've cooked something for you two to eat now to fill your empty bellies."

A tray preceded Geneviève into the room. She spoke to him as she strode through to a little dining nook next to windows which also displayed the gorgeous beach. Atarah trailed behind with a separate tray containing a pitcher filled with some type of juice and another with water. They made it to the table before Cyrus could try to help either of them.

However, he did make it in time to assist Atarah with her chair. He seated himself then reached for the juice pitcher to fill their glasses. His glass was halfway to his lips when, Geneviève tapped his shoulder.

"Let me know how you like the rum punch. I make it from my grandmother's recipe. She brought it with her when she came

69

over from Haiti. Everything I need to make more, is stocked in the pantry."

Putting the glass down without taking a sip, Cyrus nodded. "I'm sure we'll love it. Thank you."

"It's no problem." Geneviève beamed. Tucking the trays under one arm, she walked back toward the kitchen. "You two enjoy the food. I'll just tidy up in here then leave you two love birds alone."

The second she was completely in the kitchen, Atarah released her muffled giggles.

"What's wrong, Brother Cyrus? Do you not like rum punch?"

Narrowing his eyes, he used his fork to point at her. "Unless you want me to show you in every possible way that my thoughts toward you aren't brotherly, I suggest you rethink your choice of words."

Rolling her eyes, Atarah picked up her own fork stabbing a piece of the grilled fish onto the tines.

"Spoiledsport," she muttered.

"Nope. Just honest."

Cyrus stared at her until she glanced up from her plate to see him. The heated look he sent her, clearly projected just how unbrotherly his feelings were concerning his wife. He watched the flush creep into her face before she dipped her head, intensely focusing on her food. Releasing a low chuckle, he began eating as well.

"This really is good." Atarah smacked her lips with a light popping sound after taking a sip of her rum punch. "I'd be careful though. I saw her make it. She used the entire bottle of rum."

"Not too much of that. I don't want you falling out on me while we're on the beach."

Staring at him through slitted eyes, Atarah picked up her glass, taking a generous gulp of the contents. Watching, Cyrus waited for her to put it down.

"Did that make you feel better?"

"Maybe." Tipping her nose in the air, the woman had the nerve to sniff at him.

"So, defying me gives you a rush?" Cyrus watched her every move and micro expression.

"How is enjoying my drink defying you? *You* aren't the boss of me, Cyrus Lauder."

Putting his fork down again, Cyrus tented his hands above his plate. "Are we about to have another argument because I suggested you go easy on the liquor to keep you safe on the beach?"

"You didn't make a suggestion. You gave an order."

"Woman..."

"Man."

Releasing what he hoped was a calming breath, Cyrus clasped his hands together.

"Let me try this again."

Atarah's regal head tilt was her only acknowledgement of his olive branch.

"I was thinking we'd go down to the beach in a little while. The sun is blazing out there. So, maybe we should take it easy on the alcohol."

Unfolding her arms, Atarah picked up her fork, spearing another piece of her fish.

"A walk on the beach sounds nice."

Then, as if she hadn't nearly bitten his head off, she picked up her water glass and took a sip. For the rest of the meal, it was as if their little dust up never occurred. Neither of them touched the rum punch. Although from the smell alone, Cyrus knew it was as delicious as Atarah had made it sound.

It took a little convincing, but once they were done with their meal, they changed into bathing suits for their walk on the beach. Atarah's original reasoning for keeping on the flowing two-piece short set was that it wasn't advised to go into the water so soon after a meal. He shot her reasoning down with the assurance they'd walk for at least a half an hour before even considering going into the water. Even then, they'd likely not do more than get their feet wet.

"If we're just getting our feet wet, why can't I keep on what I have on?"

"Because it's the beach, and if we go out farther, your clothes will be heavy when they get wet."

"How do you even know I have bathing suits with me? It's not like you told me where we were going."

Although she'd been almost as reluctant as her cousin, Cyrus had recruited Iva to help him make sure Atarah had everything she needed packed for a tropical island honeymoon.

"I'm sure you have a suit. Iva took care of it for you. Now, can you get changed so we can go outside and play?"

Turning on her heel, she stalked into the closet to go through her suitcase. It took them almost a half an hour before they walked out of the sliding glass doors then onto their private beach. Only after she found the perfect cover up for the one-piece bathing suit which was cut high on the hip and low near the breasts. She was properly scandalized at Iva's choice, but Cyrus's mouth was watering.

The cover-up was their compromise as they embarked on their first activity outside their temporary home. He was learning a great deal about his wife, whether she knew she was revealing it or not. He was also seeing different things in himself. This was the first official day of their honeymoon. And, despite their tiffs, he already knew he would dread going back to the real world once it was done.

# Chapter Twelve

Atarah was seated at her desk in her home office going over the text for the sermon she planned for the coming Sunday. She and Cyrus had been back from their honeymoon for a month. What is more, she was finally settling into her new living arrangement. Although she'd prepared to move in with him before the wedding, actually doing so was still a major adjustment.

Of course, there were movers hired to do the bulk of the work. Any packing of non-precious or personal items was handled by the service. Any furniture she didn't want to take with her was donated to the Gentle Hands Domestic abuse shelter. There was always a need for such things when people were trying to rebuild their lives after losing everything.

Cyrus's home...*Their* home was actually constructed with space for two home offices. He'd already settled into the one on the first floor, so she took the one on the second, which overlooked the backyard and the pool. Before Atarah moved in, he hadn't used the space. It contained furniture that looked straight out of the guidebook to teach realtors how to make a room look attractive to potential buyers.

She'd held onto the bookshelf, the overstuffed chair and ottoman. Instead of donating the one from her old home office, she took it to the church. It fit in perfectly with the other furniture in her office there.

Looking up from reading the same passage for the fifth time, Atarah put down her pen then stood from the desk. Her mind wasn't into the task. It was only Tuesday, so she had time to get herself together and get it done. Even though weeks had passed since their honeymoon, the memories of their time on the island infiltrated her thoughts.

The Cyrus she met at their private villa on Turks and Caicos wasn't at all what she expected based on their previous relationship. He remained as stubborn as ever, but he was attentive. Thoughtful. They rarely rang for Geneviève to make breakfast, because he seemed to enjoy feeding her. She woke more than one morning to him bringing her breakfast in bed.

When they finally ventured out to explore other parts of the island, he was engaging with the people they encountered. At times, his personality bordered on gregarious, which was in stark contrast to the serious business man who occupied the other end of the conference table during their meetings with the church board.

He even took her dancing, something she hadn't done in years. Dating was dicey *before* she went into the ministry. Afterwards, it became downright weird. Men's entire demeanors changed once they learned she was a minister. They either became holier than thou or so nervous, she'd end the dates abruptly. There was no middle ground.

Cyrus definitely didn't fall victim to either of those categories. The way he looked at her, touched her, and spoke to her, said he saw her as a woman first. A woman he desired. Simply thinking of the way he played her body like a skilled musician had her pacing her office in an attempt to calm her raging libido.

On her third pass in front of the desk, her cell phone pinged with a notification. Turning toward the sound, Atarah flipped it over to look at the screen. Seeing the new message from Iva, she rounded the desk to sit. Iva was typically busy during the day. So, she normally called after work. Sparingly, she'd call when she took her lunch break.

Atarah's antenna went up as she tapped the screen to comply with her cousin's request to call at her earliest convenience. It had to be important for Iva to ask, as it was barely ten a.m. Answering the phone on the first ring, Iva didn't give Atarah a chance to question what was wrong.

"Rah-rah! Girl!"

Sitting up straighter, Atarah leaned forward. Pushing her notebook aside, she placed her elbows on the desk.

"I just got off the phone with my mama. Tell me why she's calling me all the way from Memphis to ask me if I know where Addy is."

"Addy? As in Adina? My sister?" Atarah's heart beat picked up. Anxiety put a slight tremor in her fingers, making holding the phone difficult.

"Addy's missing?" The question left Atarah's mouth in a whisper of disbelief laced with a shout of concern.

"That was my question to mama. And, before you get yourself worked up, no, she's not missing. She left her husband."

"She did what! She left Ernest?"

This time, there was no whispering. Her shout could likely be heard on most of the second floor of the house. But, since she was there alone, Atarah wasn't worried about bothering anyone.

"Yep. As of two weeks ago. Left then had him served the day after." Popping the 'P' on the word yep, Iva answered her question a mite too cheerfully for Atarah, but she didn't dwell on it. There were more pressing matters than digging into her cousin being happy Adina left Ernest.

"Wait! Had him served? As in divorce papers? That was quick." Atarah leaned into the high back of her office chair, using her toe to swivel it slightly.

"Quick?" Atarah heard the distinct sound of Iva sucking her teeth. "Girl please. You say quick. I say, she had those papers drawn up and ready a long time before she packed a bag."

Nodding in silent agreement, Atarah turned the chair until she could see the view of the backyard. She hadn't seen or talked to her sister in almost a decade. Once Atarah announced she was going to seminary, things had gotten tense between them. After she accepted her first associate pastor position, contact became virtually non-existent—which was why moving away from Clover, Tennessee wasn't a hardship. It wasn't like she had any family there any longer.

"So, why does your mama think you know where Adina is?"

Silence was the veil thrown over the call. Atarah didn't even hear her cousin breathing.

"Iv... why does your mother think you know where Addy is? Have the two of you been talking?"

Growing up, Iva had been more like their middle sister than their cousin. A year older than Atarah and a year younger than Adina, she fit perfectly into the role.

"Probably because Adina reaches out every blue moon. I haven't blocked her number the way I have some of those other hypocrites from Clover."

Lifting an eyebrow, Atarah gave her reflection in the window the skeptical expression she wanted to give her cousin.

"And that's the *only* reason."

"Well, it might be because the last time I saw her in person I told her when she was ready to leave that lying sack of shit in a three-piece suit to give me a call. I'd buy the plane ticket and put her up in a place where he couldn't find her."

"Iva!"

"What?"

"Don't, 'what', me. You know what. Of course they think you know where she is if you announced you'd help her escape in front of people."

"Girl, that was almost six years ago. Who knew they'd still remember?"

Shaking her head, Atarah made a tsking sound. "You know their memories are long when it comes to us outcasts and rebels."

"I'll accept being called a rebel, but *I'm* not an outcast. They didn't throw *me* out. I left. When I got accepted into my first-choice college in Atlanta, I knew I was never going back."

Iva's emphasis on her not being thrown out would've stung even a few years ago. Now, Atarah let it roll off her back. It was true. Her parents—her family—had essentially thrown her out for, in their opinion, going against God's will by stepping into a role designated for men only. Then to add insult to injury, she was pastoring at churches which were inclusive of *all* people. People her staunch upbringing had tried to teach her were abominations.

"You can split hairs all you want, Ivs. But, you know they have memories like elephants when it comes to what they consider disrespect. And offering to help a man's wife leave him, is the height of disrespect."

"Whatever. I'm just happy she actually got away from that troll. His two-hundred-year-old ass was sucking the life out of her."

The giggles escaped before Atarah could suppress them. "You know Ernest isn't that old."

"He acts like it. Hell, I think he was born sixty-two years old and just kept getting more geriatric by the day."

Not trying to control her laughter, Atarah wiped tears of mirth from the corners of her eyes.

"You're a mess."

A beep interrupted Iva's response. Looking at the phone, Atarah noted it was coming from the church.

"Hey, Ivs. Let me call you back. This is someone from the church."

"That's fine. I was done anyway. Go save the day."

Clicking off with her cousin, Atarah switched over to the new call.

"Hello?"

"Pastor Lauder, this is Sister Norma. There's someone here at the church asking for you."

Although it wasn't uncommon for people to show up requesting to see her, it was unusual for Atarah to receive a phone call about it. Most often, she was there when it happened. When she wasn't, the person was given a time to return or informed of her normal office hours.

For a moment, she thought it might be Adina. But she brushed the thought aside. With a standing offer from Iva, Addy wouldn't come to Atarah first. Not when she'd firmly towed the party line after their parents went no contact.

"Did they give you any information? Or did they just ask to see me?"

Norma's voice lowered then Atarah heard shuffling noises.

"She says she's your sister. What would you like me to tell her, pastor?"

Atarah was momentarily mute. She knew Norma wouldn't give out any personal information. She was also certain her secretary was curious as to why her sister wouldn't have a way to contact her other than showing up at the church on a weekday.

"Um...Please show her to the waiting area in the outer office. I'll be there shortly."

With her mind whirling with questions, Atarah gathered her purse and shoes. She wasn't sure what to expect when she came face to face with the sibling she hadn't seen or spoken to in almost ten years, but she would find out soon.

Chapter Thirteen

Cyrus flipped the cover closed on the electronic tablet he used for note-taking during meetings. People were filing out of the room and he was moving at his own pace trying to decide if he was going to stay in the office or work from home the remainder of the day.

He didn't use to be so easily distracted. However, knowing Atarah was there made it difficult not to think about cutting his day short. Since they'd returned from their honeymoon, he hadn't been able to adjust to not seeing her whenever he wanted during the day.

It wasn't even as if they'd stayed glued to one another's side the entirety of their time away. But not having her a room away was an adjustment. At least she had already been prepared to move into the house they now shared. So, there was no argument there. Her house was barely on the market a few days before it was rented out.

They both agreed, since there were no restrictions in the homeowner's association bylaws, it was better to turn the place into a rental property than to sell it. Considering Atarah was a comptroller for a real estate company before she became a full-time pastor, she was well versed in such things.

"Do you know you checked your watch fifteen times during that forty-five-minute meeting?"

Apparently *everyone* hadn't filed out of the room. Cyrus looked up to see Caleb leaning against the doorjamb. Temporarily reverting to his fourteen-year-old self, Cyrus wanted to smack the back of Caleb's head to remove the smirk from his face.

"What's your point?" Cyrus stood with his folio in one hand and his drink tumbler in the other. He needed both hands full to avoid following through with his urge.

"My point is, you couldn't have made it more obvious that you wanted to be anywhere but here. Do you even remember anything we discussed?"

Striding toward the door as if his brother wasn't blocking the exit, Cyrus brushed him off.

"If you were observing me closely enough to count the number of times I checked my watch, you should've also seen me writing notes."

"For all I know, you could've been sitting down there writing love notes to your wife."

Stepping out into the hallway, Caleb made room for Cyrus to pass, then fell into step with him, walking toward the double doors leading into their office suites.

"What's the matter, Caleb? You jealous?" Entering the suite, Cyrus continued to his office, knowing Caleb was following him.

"Jealous? Why would I be jealous?"

Rounding his desk, Cyrus put the items down, freeing his hands once more.

"You tell me. You're the one fixated on my attention to the time and whether I'm writing messages to my wife instead of taking notes on the potential acquisitions the team presented this morning. Because, if I was pouring my heart out to her, I would've missed Brooks trying to gloss over the heavy losses for the small chain of boutiques he was pitching as a way for us to diversify our holdings."

Plopping into the chair on the opposite side of Cyrus's desk, Caleb shot him a sour glance.

"Okay. Fine. So you *were* listening. It still doesn't excuse you checking your watch so much. A few months ago, if anyone in the room had done something like that, you would've stopped the meeting to ask if they had somewhere else to be."

"I'm not that big of an asshole."

Cyrus's rebuttal was met with Caleb's knowing expression. "Fine, I'm an asshole. I still say I wouldn't have stopped the meeting to ask. I'm an asshole, not a bully."

"Tell that to your new wife."

Caleb leaned back in the chair, folding his hands together across his chest. He made the seat look like it was extremely comfortable. Cyrus knew for a fact it wasn't. He'd purposely asked the designer for chairs which were moderately comfortable, but didn't invite long visits. With Caleb being the same height as him, Cyrus was certain the chair wasn't nearly as cozy as he made it out to be.

"I don't have to tell my wife anything. She knows who I am."

"Sure she does." Caleb closed his eyes.

If Cyrus didn't know better, he'd swear his brother was intending to take a nap. However, Caleb's words jolted him.

"What the hell is that supposed to mean?" Cyrus ground his teeth then rethought his decision not to smack Caleb's head.

Waving a hand without opening his eyes, Caleb continued as if he didn't hear the threat in Cyrus's voice.

"Don't worry about it. I'm just glad you finally did something instead of pulling her hair, picking fights like you two were in grade school and not full-grown adults."

"Fuck you."

"No thanks. That's called incest. Even if it wasn't, I'm not into dudes."

Shooting his brother a death glare wouldn't make a bit of difference. So, Cyrus rolled his chair into position and sat down. A nudge to the mouse woke the computer, bringing his monitor to life. As if Caleb wasn't sitting less than ten feet away, Cyrus concentrated on the screen. Only his brother wouldn't be so easily ignored.

"Jill said you don't have any meetings for the rest of the day. Maybe if you go home and get it out of your system, you can focus the rest of the week."

Cutting him a glare, Cyrus put his attention back on his monitor. "Notice how I didn't ask for your advice on what to do with the rest of my day? That's because I don't care to hear your thoughts on my personal life."

Opening one eye, Caleb peered at him. "So, to spite me, you're going to sit over there suffering when you know you want to go home to be with your new wife."

Closing his eye again, he shifted in the chair. "I really am starting to think you were dropped on your head more than that one time mom told us about."

Picking up the earth shaped stress ball from his desk, Cyrus sent it flying toward Caleb hitting him directly in the center of his forehead. Jolting upright, Caleb glared at him.

"Don't take your frustration out on me. Just go home." Grabbing the blue and green-colored ball, he threw it back toward Cyrus who caught it in one hand.

"My only source of frustration at the moment is you." Cyrus once again attempted to ignore his brother.

There was absolutely no way he would admit how right Caleb was about him wanting to be home with Atarah. Even though he knew she was working herself and could possibly be called away at any moment because of an issue at the church or with one of the congregants.

The buzzing from his phone drew his attention away from his increasingly annoying younger brother. Checking the display, he recognized the number as one of the board members. Nice man, but a bit of a gossip. Still, it was rare for him to call, so Cyrus answered.

"Lauder."

"Brother Cyrus, this is Perry Carruthers. From the church."

Resisting the urge to roll his eyes, Cyrus managed to keep his tone even when he responded.

"Yes, Brother Perry. I recognize your voice." He held back from asking any leading questions.

Leading questions tended to end with being volunteered for unwanted tasks or an endless conversation listening to someone's woes. Cyrus did what he wanted, when he wanted. Guilt trips no longer had a place in his life. So, he waited for Perry to reveal the reason for the call.

"Okay, well I'm sure you might be busy. So, I'll get right to it. I don't want to gossip, but I'm at the church. Some strange woman just showed up asking about the pastor, saying she's the pastor's sister. Pastor Cox—"

"Lauder." Cyrus interrupted to correct the man.

"Right. Apologies. Pastor Lauder has been here over two years and the only family I've ever seen is a cousin. Now, don't get me wrong, the woman looks nice enough. But when the pastor showed up, she didn't look like her normal self. She looked a mite worried."

Standing, Cyrus tapped his pockets to be certain he had his keys. Locking his computer, he left it sitting on the docking station as he rounded his desk. Caleb frowned, mouthing to him to ask what was going on.

"Thank you for letting me know, Brother Perry. I appreciate your concern. I'm certain everything is fine."

"You're welcome. I just thought, if it were me I'd wanna know about some stranger coming around upsetting my wife."

Rushing the other man off the phone without feeding into his penchant for gossip, Cyrus strode from his office with Caleb on his heels. Not sparing his brother a glance, Cyrus tossed out instructions to their assistant Jill.

"I'm leaving for the rest of the day. Don't forward my calls. They can leave a message or call me back tomorrow."

Nodding in understanding, Jill continued to type away on her keyboard.

"Same goes for me."

Barely turning his head to look at Caleb, Cyrus cocked one eyebrow.

"I don't need a keeper." The gruff edge of his voice said otherwise, but Cyrus didn't acknowledge the potential lie.

"Yeah...I'm coming anyway. You have your *kick ass and don't take names* look on your face."

Arguing with Caleb would require energy Cyrus didn't want to expend. Although his brother was only partially right about the expression on his face. He didn't believe in putting his hands on a woman, but he couldn't trust himself if one of Atarah's family members had shown up to give her shit.

As far as he knew, Iva was the closest person she had to a sister since her immediate family had essentially disowned her. Whatever this so-called sister wanted from his wife was bound to cause Atarah some kind of heartache or strife. Cyrus wouldn't stand for it.

# Chapter Fourteen

Atarah didn't break any speed limits to reach the church, but she still made it there within twenty minutes. Absently greeting one of the board members on her way inside, she worked to calm the thundering of her heart. Despite Iva telling her about Adina leaving her husband, it was a shock to her system for her sister to show up at Harmony Haven.

It hadn't occurred to her what she'd do if she was to ever be face-to-face with her immediate family again. She'd resolved herself to living the remainder of her days without them. Now, she wasn't certain if this was an opportunity for herself or something else. Like Adina using her, since no one would believe Atarah would be the person her older sister would turn to in time of need.

Taking a calming breath, Atarah pushed open the door to the waiting area outside her office. The moment she stepped over the threshold her gaze landed on Adina. Dressed in jeans, a t-shirt and sneakers with her thick hair gathered into a high ponytail, her sister looked like she was ready for a day of going thrifting then craft fair shopping.

Adina popped up from the chair like it was on fire. Her steps faltered after only making two without Atarah moving closer to her. Neither of them said anything—not even a stiff formal greeting.

Norma finally broke the silence. "Hello, Pastor Lauder."

Breaking eye contact with her sister, Atarah turned her gaze onto her secretary. Pulling up a smile, she attempted to put her at ease.

"Good morning, Norma. I hope your day has been going well."

Although she looked confused about Atarah's general greeting, and lack of one to her guest, Norma responded with the usual pleasantries about her morning answering calls and going through the assignments she'd been given.

"Atarah." Adina's voice was soft. Tentative. "Atarah, can I speak with you please?"

Once again turning her attention to her sister, Atarah knew she couldn't continue to use Norma as a shield. Extending her arm, she pointed toward the door to her office.

"In my office."

With a nod to Norma, Atarah opened the door, then waited until Adina was inside before closing it behind her. Walking around her desk, she pulled out the rolling chair. Pointing to the tufted seats opposite the desk, she invited Adina to sit.

Her sister's hands were clasped together with her fingers gripping so hard her knuckles were several shades lighter than the toasted brown of the rest of her skin. As they had in the waiting area, neither of them spoke.

It was a tad spiteful, but Atarah refused to break the ice. She'd tried that many times over the years. Stopping once it became clear her sister didn't want to be her sister any longer.

Ultimately, Adina broke the silence. "I'm sorry, Rah-rah."

Closing her eyes against the onslaught of emotions in addition to the memories evoked with the utterance of the nickname only Adina and Iva had ever called her, Atarah fought to keep her emotions in check. When her eyelids lifted, Adina was staring at her. A sheen of unshed tears glistened in her sister's eyes.

"Is that why you came here? To say sorry? What exactly are you sorry for, Adina?"

Unlike her sister, Atarah didn't toss around nicknames. Her sister had made herself a stranger to her. So, there would be no lapses into informality as if they were still close.

Adina's sharp inhale was accompanied by one hand flying to her chest. Her expression said Atarah may as well as slapped her face. Calling her by her given name had the same effect.

"Everything. I'm sorry for everything, Rah-rah. Not standing up to daddy and mama. Not supporting you regardless of what they said. Not being brave enough to follow what I know is right. Not fighting harder to save our friendship our sister bond...Everything."

The tears finally spilled from Adina's eyes, streaking her face with wetness. Swiping them away seemed to do no good, since a fresh line would immediately appear.

A boulder sat on Atarah's vocal cords. Bees stung the backs of her eyes. She'd waited so long, but never thought she'd hear any type of acknowledgement of the damage done to their relationship. In particular, the hope of an apology had long died. Now, her sister sat before her with an opportunity. Hurt wouldn't allow Atarah to simply jump on it without question.

"Why? Why now? Why did you come now? Was it because you left Ernest, and now you need a place to hide where no one will think to look for you?"

Although, she didn't think she intended it, Atarah's voice sounded snide to her own ears.

Pulling her body up ramrod straight in the visitor's chair, Adina took another swipe at the wetness on her face.

"No. And I'm not hiding. I just didn't announce to those lying hypocrites where I was going—especially not Ernest."

Beneath the scorn laced into her words, Atarah heard Adina's pain as well. Whether it was from her years counseling people or their previously close relationship, but she heard it. The sound tugged at her heart strings a little harder. However, she still needed answers.

"Why then? What made you come to me now?"

"That woman out there. Your secretary. Norma? She called you Pastor Lauder. Which means, I missed your wedding. Your *wedding*, Rah. Even though you couldn't stand Ernest, while knowing I was making the biggest mistake of my life, you still came to my wedding. You stood beside me. You spent a ridiculous amount of money on a dress, and all the unnecessary things mama said we just *had* to have. You never once complained.

But, I wasn't there for *you*. What's worse is I had my head so far up my ass, I didn't realize you hadn't excluded me from your day. You sent me an invitation. After everything, you still reached out to invite me to your wedding, and I didn't come."

Fresh tears cascaded down Adina's cheeks, but she didn't swipe them away.

"I don't know how long I would've stayed in the dark if I hadn't found the invitation when I was cleaning Ernest's office. I don't know why he didn't throw it away. He called himself hiding it. When I confronted him about it..."

Adina's voice trailed off. She looked away from Atarah, staring mutely out of the large bay window. Instinct told Atarah not to interrupt. Just wait. Her sister had a story to tell and she might only get the courage to tell it once. Her intuition was correct. After a few beats of silence, Adina began to talk.

And once she started, she told it all. Everything she'd uncovered after confronting her husband about the hidden invitation. From the way their parents pressured her to marry Ernest, which is why she didn't think she could say no. To the way they purposely drove a wedge between her and Atarah. To their mother telling her early in her marriage to not make a fuss if Ernest was showing one of the parishioners too much personal attention.

But the final straw, what brought the house of cards tumbling down was when Ernest had revealed the lengths they'd gone to in order to be certain the sisters each thought the other wanted nothing to do with them. She glossed over Ernest's jibes about her being so young and unable to give him children. Adina seemed relieved to not have born her husband's spawn.

No. It was when she understood her parents and husband used her to purposely isolate Atarah, that Adina said enough was enough. Iva was spot on when she said Addy had the divorce papers ready and waiting. She'd been trying to build up the courage to leave Ernest. He'd finally given her the push she needed to take the plunge.

By the time Addy reached the end of her story, Atarah had rounded the desk. The two were seated side-by-side embracing and sobbing together. They were both crying while apologizing when Cyrus burst into the office with Caleb hot on his trail.

## Chapter Fifteen

On the drive from his office to the church, Cyrus's mind created a multitude of scenarios. None of them matched what he witnessed when he stalked past Norma's desk and swung open the door to Atarah's office. The scene before him was so unanticipated, he was initially at a loss for words.

Only one of his potential expectations was a reality. His wife had tears on her face. But, they didn't match the previous image his mind conjured up. Her face wasn't contorted with pain or anger from having to defend herself. It appeared to be more of an eclectic mix of joy, sorrow and relief. From both women.

Caleb bumping into his back forced Cyrus to step farther into the room. Releasing herself from the other woman's hold, Atarah stood with her hands raised and her palms facing outward. He couldn't be certain if it was to ward him off or in anticipation of what was to come. Because, he immediately wrapped her in his arms.

Although he'd only seen her sister in a few old photos when Atarah was unpacking her things, Cyrus immediately recognized her. The sisters shared similar facial structures, but varied in the skin tone. Adina's gaze was locked onto the two of them. He was certain she noticed the way Atarah seemed to cling to him as he held her.

Race had never been an issue between him and Atarah, but the slight widening of Adina's eyes said she was surprised about something. But, Cyrus conceded he could be reading more into the expression than was there. Atarah's muffled voice made him pull back to look into her face.

Swiping at the remaining wetness, he dried her face with his fingers.

"What was that?"

"I said. Thank you for the hug, but what are you two doing here?"

Shooting a glance over his shoulder to Caleb, Cyrus found his brother staring around the room as if he was on a museum tour, patently ignoring making eye contact. *Traitor*.

Cyrus had been so convinced of what he'd find when he showed up, he hadn't bothered to construct a plausible explanation for his sudden appearance during the late morning hours. He couldn't spill the beans about Brother Perry. He also didn't want her thinking he was having her watched. Although it was his habit to keep his finger on the pulse of what was happening in most areas of his life.

Going with a partial truth, he replied, "I came to see you."

Atarah's frown said he wasn't going to get off so easily with his simple response.

"But, how did you know I was here? I told you I was working from home today."

The joy he would've felt from hearing her refer to their house as home was tamped down by how quickly she turned things around with another question. Before he could scramble to come up with another viable answer, her thoughts spilled forth.

"Did Norma call you too? I didn't ask her to do that. I know she was worried, but it wasn't necessary for her to get you all worked up."

Despite the rush of relief he felt when she latched onto another plausible explanation, he couldn't let Norma take the blame. They were still building their relationship dynamic. He didn't want her putting Norma in the same category with Celia.

"No, baby. Norma didn't call me. Why don't we talk about it later and you tell me what all the tears were about?"

When Atarah looked over her shoulder toward her sister, Cyrus was thankful he'd managed to redirect the conversation. Besides, how he knew she potentially needed him didn't matter. What mattered was that she did, and he was there.

Totally oblivious to what her touch did to him, Atarah's hands skimmed down his chest before she tangled their fingers together then turned to face her sister. As enthralled as he was by his wife, Cyrus didn't miss the way the other woman's gaze was glued to their joined digits.

"Cy, this is my sister Adina Cox-Smith. Adina, this is my husband Cyrus Lauder."

Lessons from his mother wouldn't allow him to simply stare at Adina—even if he was suspicious of her sudden appearance. So, he extended his hand as she stood.

"Hello, Mrs. Cox-Smith."

"Please. Just call me Adina." Accepting his offer, she shook his hand briefly, releasing it almost as quickly as she grasped it.

"Ok, Adina. Feel free to call me Cyrus."

Not even Caleb called him Cy. Atarah had started it while they were on their honeymoon, and he discovered he liked it—when it came from her. He'd always rejected the shorted form of his name previously. His acceptance might have something to do with her moaning it in his ear during one of their countless rounds of lovemaking.

The fingers of Atarah's free hand squeezed his bicep as she leaned into him slightly. "To answer your question, Adina and I were having a sister moment. The tears were a by-product."

"A sister moment?"

Cyrus's gaze pinged between his wife and her sister before coming back to study Atarah's upturned face.

"Yes. A sister moment. It's been..." She paused, looking at Adina before returning his stare once again. "A while since we last saw each other or spoke. Things got a bit emotional."

Cupping the side of her face, Cyrus rubbed his thumb along her cheek.

"So, those were happy tears? Because those are the only ones you're allowed to shed without me tearing some shit up."

"Cyrus! We're in the church!"

"Technically, we're in the office. Not the sanctuary."

Her combination frown and pout were cute, even if she was trying to get on to him.

"Don't split hairs." She attempted to scold him.

"Don't act like you haven't cussed a blue streak in this very office."

Atarah had the audacity to look embarrassed he'd mentioned her penchant for using profanity was comparable to his.

Throat clearing drew their attention to Caleb, saving his wife from addressing the truth of Cyrus's statement. Rolling his eyes, Cyrus jerked a thumb over his shoulder pointing to his brother.

"Excuse my manners, Adina. This is my brother, Caleb."

Once Cyrus said his name, Caleb moved closer extending his hand. Adina accepted it, but while they shook, a different expression took over her face.

"That's it! That's why you look so familiar!"

Cyrus and Caleb exchanged confused glances before regarding her with curious stares. It was Atarah who spoke the question aloud.

"They look familiar? From where?"

"Little Shepherds."

"Little Shepherds?" Atarah's brow furrowed matching the new expression on Cyrus's face. It had been more than twenty years since he'd thought about that place.

"Yes! You probably don't remember, because you were with the younger kids, but he was a counselor one year. And he," Adina pointed to Caleb, "was a troublemaker. He was always getting sent back to his cabin to read scripture and *think about his actions.*"

The last part, Adina put in air quotes. Although it had been years, Cyrus remembered the last summer he spent as a counselor at Little Shepherds camp. Adina was correct, Caleb was always getting sent back to the cabins. At which point, he would promptly slip away to their grandparent's house on the other side of the lake.

Somehow, he always managed to make it back before anyone other than Cyrus noticed he was gone. Tilting his head to the side, Cyrus's brow furrowed. He didn't recall meeting Atarah or Adina at camp. Although with the age difference between them, Atarah's first year would've been his last. So, they wouldn't have had much opportunity to interact.

If he recalled correctly, her sister was two years older. The odds were better that they'd have overlap, yet he couldn't place the current face of the woman with any of the teenaged girls he remembered from so long ago. Apparently, his confusion was painted clearly on his face.

"At camp, I almost exclusively went by Addy. No one ever called me Adina."

Cyrus still couldn't place her, but Caleb spoke up when she mentioned her nickname.

"Address Addy?" The questioning lilt in his voice was tinged with humor.

"You would remember that insult wouldn't you, Cable?" The way Adina spoke to his brother made Cyrus think she was going to stick her tongue out at him. Purposely mispronouncing his name seemed to intrigue Caleb even more.

"Well, isn't this a small world?" Caleb slid his hands in his pockets and Cyrus looked back at his wife whose face was coated with the same confusion he felt.

Their silent discussion was interrupted by a rumbling sound which had everyone staring at Caleb.

"According to my belly clock, it's time for lunch. Are you ladies hungry? We can grab something. Cyrus's treat."

Cyrus's expression melted into the glare he sent his brother. "I never said I was buying you food."

"You brought me here at lunch time. What did you expect?"

"Brought you? I didn't bring you anywhere. You invited yourself."

A gentle squeeze to his fingers pulled Cyrus back from laying into Caleb.

"I *am* hungry."

That's all Atarah said. But it's all he needed to hear. Dismissing Caleb, Cyrus invited Adina to share the meal with them. Once she accepted, he escorted them to his vehicle. Shooting his brother a warning glare, Cyrus helped Atarah into the rear since she wanted to sit next to her sister on the drive.

# Chapter Sixteen

This day definitely wasn't going as Atarah planned. Instead of constructing her sermon for the upcoming Sunday then reviewing the scripture for the series they were discussing in bible study, she was seated at a trendy restaurant. On one side of her, was the sister she hadn't spoken to in years. On the other, was her husband, who was watching them like they were going to reveal the secrets of the universe at any moment, and he didn't want to miss it.

The normal level of attention she received from Cyrus seemed to be on overload. He was hyper focused. It was clear he'd accepted what she told him in her office, but he maintained a healthy distrust of Adina's sudden appearance.

Of the many things which had changed or softened following their rushed marriage, one thing about him remained the same. Cyrus was skeptically observant. Between shooting Caleb warning glances, he seemed to be mentally making note of everything Adina and Atarah said to one another.

Trying to shake off the possibility that he'd seen something she hadn't, in regard to her sister, Atarah put her attention on the menu. While she was hungry, she had no idea what she wanted to eat. So, when the waiter first stopped at their table, she tried to go last with placing her order in an effort to force herself to choose. Cyrus wouldn't have it. He prompted everyone to at least enter drink orders before giving instructions to the young man.

"We'll have the appetizer sampler to start. But, we'll need a few more minutes before we order the entrées. Thank you."

While his words were polite, his take charge manner put a hard edge to his voice—which could be construed as rude. Yet another thing she'd begun to understand. She'd fallen victim to that misconception, putting them on the wrong foot almost from the beginning of her time at Harmony Haven.

Leaning closer to Cyrus, Atarah touched his arm. Attempting to keep their conversation private was useless, but she tried anyway.

"I really would've settled on something by the time the rest of you ordered. You didn't have to send him away."

"It's fine. Besides, it's bad manners for me to go before you."

Shaking her head, her brow furrowed gently. "Who knew you were such a gentleman?"

"You would've known it sooner if you hadn't been so hell bent on fighting me all the time."

The dip in Atarah's brow deepened. "I beg your pardon." Tossing her most recent thought out of the window, she squared her shoulders, ready to defend her position.

"I wasn't hell bent on fighting you. You just didn't like that you couldn't run over me like you did Reverend Marshall."

Atarah had heard from multiple sources that the kindly older man would agree with whatever the board decided, and seemed to have no real plans of his own. She could believe it. Though their interaction was brief before he retired, turning the church over to her, she'd recognized he was quick to go along with whatever she suggested.

"No one ran over Reverend Marshall. He just understood how the board worked. He trusted us to act in the best interest of the church."

"Are you two about to start fighting? If you are, can you wait until the appetizer gets here? I like to eat while I'm being entertained."

Cyrus glared at his brother. Atarah sat up straight in her seat, smoothing the edge of her shirt. Caleb's comment had snapped her back into the reality of where they were and that they weren't alone.

As much as she stepped away from some of the teachings of her childhood, she still held to some. Since they'd married, no matter the circumstances which brought about the union, she didn't argue with him in front of other people. Atarah made a concerted effort to keep their disagreements private. When they were together, they were a united front.

"We aren't fighting. And mind your own business."

Cyrus's gruff reprimand of Caleb might as well have been a gnat buzzing around the other man's head. He brushed it off then bantered back with the same quick wit.

"I don't know if you missed the part of biology class when they talked about what the eyes and the ears do. But, when you do things directly in front of other people, they can see them. They can also hear them. So, it is my business if you're doing it less than three feet away from me."

Before Cyrus could counter his brother's quip, Adina chimed in.

"I see you're still a troublemaker. Funny how nothing has changed in the last twenty-five years."

Shifting his focus from Cyrus to Adina, Caleb grinned. "So, you've been counting the days since you last saw me? I'm flattered."

Adina's face scrunched like she smelled something foul. "What? No. But, I do know math. It's not hard, even when you don't use your fingers. Just don't forget to carry the one."

Atarah's gaze pinged between the two. She sincerely had no memory of either brother from camp, but apparently, Adina and Caleb got to know each other that summer. It was both girls' first time since their parents hadn't wanted to send Adina until Atarah was old enough to attend as well.

Their chatter broke the momentary strain developing between Atarah and Cyrus, allowing her to return her attention to the menu. Although she was hungry, nothing really caught her eye. So, she opted for the Caesar salad. It was her go-to when she didn't have a taste for anything in particular.

By the time, the waiter returned with their drinks, everyone was ready to order entrées. Atarah pulled out her diplomacy skills. Her situation with Cyrus notwithstanding, Atarah was good at guiding a conversation to more pleasant topics. Or at least different ones. Considering how long it had been since she'd spoken to Adina, most topics of conversation contained emotional landmines. So, it was a tall order.

The safest topic seemed to be discussing her recent trip to Turks and Caicos. Artfully skirting the amount of time she and Cyrus spent inside their villa exploring one another's bodies, Atarah regaled her sister with stories of the island's beauty. She gushed over how much she enjoyed discovering the different foods. The server picked that moment to bring the appetizer platter containing crab puffs, fried cheese, spinach stuffed pastries, with pan seared shrimp.

The moment he placed it on the center of the table, Atarah recoiled. She wasn't a huge fan of spinach, and it smelled particularly pungent—even while wrapped in the pastry.

"Is something wrong?" Cyrus's question made Atarah fix her face as she shook her head.

"No. I'm not a spinach fan." Waving her hand for them to continue, she took a sip of her water to combat the slight nausea the scent inspired.

Following their own individual blessing of the food, the others portioned their selections on the small plates provided. Atarah opted for the rolls the waiter brought out with their drinks.

The warming hand Cyrus placed on her leg, drew Atarah's gaze to his. Turning toward him, she silently questioned him with her lifted eyebrow.

"Are you sure you're okay? You said you were hungry. There's more than the spinach on the platter."

"I'm fine. I'm eating. See."

She made a show of taking a generous bite of the bread she'd been consuming in small pinching bites. Cyrus looked like he wanted to say more, but he clamped his lips closed, returning to his food. When Atarah looked up again, she met her sister's assessing gaze.

Giving Adina an expression similar to the one she'd given Cyrus, Atarah mouthed, "what?" Shaking her head, Adina went back to eating her crab puff. Atarah nearly moaned in gratitude when the last spinach pastry disappeared from Caleb's plate and the waiter came to take the platter away.

They'd timed it perfectly, since their entrées were ready. The salad she ordered looked amazing. She could tell they hadn't skimped by giving her the less desirable parts of the lettuce. The restaurant portions were generous. They'd even supplied two ramakins of salad dressing instead of the customary one.

With her stomach finally resettled, Atarah poured both small containers over the greens and mixed the dressing in. At her first bite, her face crumpled. Immediately spitting it into her napkin, she began inspecting her food.

"Is something wrong with your salad?" This time it was Caleb asking the question.

"I don't know if it's the lettuce, the chicken, or the salad dressing, but something tastes off." Atarah continued to move around the contents of the bowl looking for any signs of one of the ingredients having gone bad.

# Chapter Seventeen

Once Atarah spit out the first bite of the salad he'd ordered to replace the one she had before, Cyrus knew something was definitely wrong. He didn't know what, but he knew something wasn't right. From the look on his newly discovered sister-in-law's face, she'd noticed as well. However, he'd learned that pressuring his wife would get him exactly nowhere—unless he wanted her to stop talking to him altogether.

By the time her second salad arrived, everyone else was nearly done with their meal. She'd insisted they not stop eating simply because she didn't have her food. So, Cyrus settled the bill, and they left.

"I still think we should stop somewhere to get you something or call in an order to a place near the house. Those two little pieces of bread aren't enough for lunch."

"I'm fine, Cy. I'll find something at the house. Don't worry about it."

Rather than continue to go back and forth on the subject, Cyrus fell silent. After a few minutes, the sisters began a quiet conversation about Logan City with Adina asking how her sister liked living in the area. Listening with half an ear, Cyrus started a separate conversation with his own sibling. By the time they made it to the church, they had a plan all worked out.

Once he parked in a parking space near Atarah's vehicle, he passed Caleb his key fob before getting out to open the rear passenger door for his wife. The foursome stood awkwardly for a second. Finally, Cyrus nudged the conversation in the direction he wanted it to go.

Looking at his brother he tilted his head. "Don't you need to get back to the office? You can have someone drop my car off later."

"Yeah, sure..." For a change, Caleb didn't offer a snappy come-back. Nor did he remind Cyrus he'd taken the rest of the day off. Instead, he nodded to Atarah. "I hope you feel better."

"Thanks, Caleb. But, I told y'all I'm fine. It was the salad. Something was bad in it. Nothing is wrong with me." Atarah's words didn't match the dull tint her skin had taken on over the course of their lunch. However, Cyrus didn't call her out on it.

Caleb didn't look convinced either, but Cyrus was pleased his younger brother followed his lead.

"Yeah, okay. See you at the office, Cyrus." Casting a glance at Adina, Caleb winked. "Nice to see you again, Address Addy."

Adina's response to Caleb's teasing was a closed mouth along with the slight squinting of her eyes. He still didn't have vivid memories of interacting with her. Cyrus did recall Caleb mentioning someone he called Address Addy during the summer of the last time Cyrus attended the camp. The following summer, he chose early enrollment, spending those two and a half months launching his college career.

Cyrus, Atarah and Adina stood on the sidewalk leading into the office entrance of the church as Caleb climbed into the SUV.

"Cy, why is Caleb driving your truck? Are you not going back to the office? You aren't taking the rest of the day off because of me are you? I told you I'm fine."

Shaking his head, Cyrus slid an arm around her waist. "I was already planning to work from home the rest of the day. Caleb threw a wrench in my plan by hopping in with me when I left. So, since you aren't feeling well, I'll drive you back home. He's going to drop my vehicle off later. No biggie."

"But..." Atarah trailed off looking from him to her sister.

Adina seemed to catch the expression on Atarah's face at the same time as Cyrus.

"Don't worry about me. I honestly got more time with you today than I thought I would. And I'm not going anywhere. I planned to go see Iva after speaking with you."

The dip in Atarah's brow wasn't anger, but it wasn't quite hurt either. "So, is that where you're staying? With Iva?"

"No. I found a place through a mutual friend of a friend. I'll stay there until I decide what I want to do next."

As Cyrus was wondering if Adina was hiding from someone, Atarah voiced his internal concern.

"I thought you weren't hiding, Addy."

The question was simple enough, yet Cyrus noted the sheen of tears which sprang to Adina's eyes. He released his grip on Atarah to allow her to embrace her sister.

Their hug was brief, before Atarah pulled back to look at her sister. Taller by a few inches, she tilted her head down slightly to make eye contact.

"You don't have to stay with strangers. My old place is under lease, but—"

"No." Adina shook her head before Atarah could finish her sentence. Cyrus wasn't sure if he should thank her for immediately rejecting the suggestion or be suspicious that she was so quick to say no.

"What? Why not?"

"Because you're still a newlywed, Rah. You and your husband deserve this time to yourself without worrying about a house guest. Besides, your alone time is going to be limited."

Adina's single raised eyebrow preceded her words. "What's that supposed to mean?"

"Nothing. Forget I said anything."

They'd never had a conversation before this day, however Cyrus read Adina's look with eerie clarity. *Holy shit!* It was so obvious, he wondered why it hadn't occurred to him before now. Apparently, he wasn't the only clueless one in his relationship, because confusion was painted on his wife's face.

"Are you forgetting you're a full-time pastor, baby? We'd barely touched down from our honeymoon before people were calling. Even though we both know the associate pastors were here and made themselves available during your absence."

His reminder seemed to do the trick. Her face eased into a more neutral expression. Cyrus's plan wasn't to keep her in the dark, but he'd prefer more privacy before he broached the subject.

"Okay..." Atarah's voice trailed off.

Happy she didn't press the issue, Cyrus prompted the sisters to make certain they had exchanged information. He still wasn't one hundred percent sold on Adina being back in Atarah's life, but he recognized his wife was hopeful. So, he didn't want to be the reason she doubted her sister.

Once they had one another's numbers, they hugged again. Adina got into her four-door sedan then drove away while Atarah and Cyrus remained on the walkway watching.

"Is there anything you need from inside?"

"No. I guess I started walking this way out of habit. All I brought with me earlier was my purse and keys. My purse is still in my car."

Until she mentioned it, Cyrus hadn't paid attention to the fact that she didn't have anything in her hands when they went to the restaurant. Since she was with him, it wasn't as if she needed money. Still, he was surprised he hadn't noticed.

"Alright. Well, unless you want to speak to Norma, we can go home now."

Cyrus held out his hand. Atarah looked from his open palm to his face.

"Are you wanting to hold my hand or are you expecting something else?"

"Sure, we can hold hands, if that's what you want. But, pass me your keys first. Or at least unlock the doors."

Since actually putting a key into the ignition wasn't required, he didn't physically need them once the doors were unlocked.

"I'm perfectly capable of driving myself, Cyrus Lauder."

*Uh-Oh. She'd used his first and last name...* Closing the short distance between them, Cyrus peered into her face.

"I'm aware, but humor me. I want to drive my wife home."

Staring at him skeptically for a solid minute, Atarah finally reached into the pocket of her pants, retrieving the key fob. Accepting it, he held out his hand to escort her to the car. As they were leaving, he saw Brother Perry walking out of the building. Cyrus gave him a nod then a wave, but didn't stop to chat.

The last thing he needed was the older man mentioning the phone call he'd made and starting Atarah back up on why Cyrus had burst into her office earlier. As it was, he was trying to figure out how he'd break the news to his wife that she was likely pregnant with their first child.

# Chapter Eighteen

"Cyrus... Just because I got a little nauseous at lunch when I was served a couple of bad Caesar salads, doesn't mean I'm pregnant."

Atarah stared at him like he'd grown a second head with another set of arms sticking out of his sides. There was no way she was pregnant. Her breasts were sore right this minute in preparation for the period she expected to start any day now.

Besides, she'd had her period last month too—the week they got back from their honeymoon. It was light, but it was there. So, Cyrus Lauder had taken leave of his senses at worst. At best, he was wishful thinking since a few people had no respect for boundaries and hinted at them starting a family right away.

Catching her around the waist when she tried to walk past him to put the deli slices back in the refrigerator, Cyrus plucked the meat from her hand, placing it on the countertop.

"Hey, stop for a second."

"I thought you wanted me to eat something? I'm trying to make a sandwich."

Atarah didn't fight against his hold even if she didn't understand why he was suddenly so fixated on the idea that she was pregnant. The likelihood of him being correct was so slim, she didn't think a discussion was warranted.

"Of course I want you to eat, but I'm not going to let you sidestep this conversation." Squeezing her tighter, then loosening his arms, Cyrus peered into her eyes.

"Humor me for a few minutes."

Pursing her lips, Atarah lifted her eyebrows in silent consent. Apparently, Cyrus took her expression as an invitation, because he kissed her lightly before pulling away.

"It's not just about today at lunch. Last night, when I was visiting with the girls, you asked me to be gentle, saying they were sore."

Twirling her finger, Atarah motioned for him to continue. Because sore breasts were a monthly occurrence. So, he'd have to do better than that.

"Atarah...we've been married exactly forty-five days. We've been intimate nearly every one of those days."

When she started shaking her head, he added, "except one. We've gone exactly one day from the day we married without having sex. Now, I don't claim to be an expert on women's health. But shouldn't you have had at least one period by now? Unless you have one of those things that makes it stop."

His assessment gave Atarah a moment of pause. She didn't have the kind of IUD which made periods a non-issue. And she usually could set her calendar by how precisely she menstruated each month. But...even if it wasn't as heavy as usual, there was that day the week they got back from Turks and Caicos. She attributed the lightness to the stress of the move. It had happened once before where she was stressed and missed a period.

Atarah's facial muscles ticked as her expression settled into something different from the skepticism she'd worn when Cyrus first broached the subject. Her internal head shakes of denial became actual, vigorous shakes, causing her curls to bounce.

Her face must've displayed her anxiety in her denial, because Cyrus's embrace transitioned into him rubbing her back and arms.

"It's okay, baby. How about this? We'll just get a test. Then if the test doesn't convince you, we'll get an appointment with your doctor."

While he spoke, he pulled his phone from his pocket, swiping his thumb around on the screen. A few minutes passed before he placed a few decisive taps to the phone, put it back in his pocket then released her. To Atarah, it felt as if she was watching the two of them from outside her body. He released her to walk to the pantry, returning with two bottles of water and a clear, disposable cocktail cup.

Her eyes went back and forth between his face and the items in his hands. With limbs that felt weighted down, she pointed to them.

"What are those for?"

"I placed an order with Shopping Friend. I paid extra for them to get us a few tests here in less than their normal one-hour window." Setting one water bottle onto the counter along with the cup, he passed her the other. "Drink up."

Wrapping her fingers around the bottle, she took it from him. "Fine. I'll play along. But you're wrong. I'm a grown woman. I know my own body."

Okay...*So maybe Cyrus wasn't completely wrong*...Atarah stood in the bathroom after depositing a urine sample into the makeshift specimen cup her husband gave her, looking at lines appear on one test while the word *pregnant* was slowly forming on another test, as the word yes popped up on the screen of the third.

How the hell had this happened? Even as the question screamed loudly in her mind, her inner sensible self, attempted to relay the numerous times she and Cyrus had sex without giving even a thought to other forms of contraception. Atarah really didn't want to hear from her practical inner voice. Not right now.

Right now, she was on the verge of a complete freak out. Because how was she expected to navigate this situation with Cyrus if they had a baby? What would that mean for them?

The raps on the door were soft, but they might as well have been cannons battering against the wooden surface. Jumping, Atarah's head whipped around to look at it. Knowing Cyrus's penchant for knocking while walking into the room, she'd locked the door. The jiggling of the handle said she was right to think ahead.

"Hey, It's been four minutes. Why is the door locked?" His deep voice was muted by the obstruction between them, but loud enough for her to hear.

"Because I deserve to pee alone." Even as she shot her response back, she walked over to the door to unlock it.

Cyrus entered with his displeasure written in his expression. Striding over to the tests lined up on a towel on the countertop, he hovered above them. He stared at them for less than ten seconds before he whirled around to look at her.

With one hand still on the doorknob, she observed the elation coating his features. He wasn't simply happy about the possibility of her being pregnant. He was ecstatic. It begged the question...why?

While she battled internally, Cyrus swept her into his arms, raining kisses on her face only pausing to place his hands on her belly—which was round long before there was a thought of her housing a baby in her womb. His cognac-colored eyes sparkled with his obvious joy, making Atarah feel she wasn't responding appropriately to this life altering news.

It was while he was staring lovingly at where his hand lay on her stomach that he finally noticed her level of excitement didn't match his own. Lifting her chin, Atarah accepted the gentle kiss Cyrus placed on her lips. He'd relocated his hands from her abdomen to cup the sides of her face.

"Hey, what's with the face? Are you not happy? I thought you wanted children."

Wrapping her fingers around his wrists, Atarah reflexively stroked the exposed skin with her thumbs.

"I do want children. And it's not that I'm not happy. I'm just..."

Her words petered into silence as she tried to work out the right words which wouldn't sound like an accusation or as if she didn't want the potential life they'd created together. Because nothing was farther from the truth.

"It's just what?" Cyrus lowered himself until her vision was narrowed to include nothing but his face.

"You're acting like we planned this. Like we came into this marriage knowing we'd immediately start a family and live happily ever after. That's not how this happened. Any of it. I'm very confused by it all."

Atarah wanted to kick herself when some of the light faded from Cyrus's eyes. It was exactly what she didn't want. She didn't want to dull his joy.

# Chapter Nineteen

*Damnit.* Looking into Atarah's eyes, Cyrus read beyond her words. She wasn't simply confused about his joy surrounding her being pregnant with his child. She was still very uncertain about their relationship and his feelings for her. It seemed none of his actions had managed to show what he hadn't said.

Clasping her hand in his, he led her from the bathroom to the sitting area of their bedroom.

"Come. Sit. Let's talk about it."

Atarah offered no objection. She simply sat on the lover's sofa with her gaze trained on him. Sitting next to her, Cyrus took her hands in his. He knew the ball was in his court. She'd been brave. Twice. Coming right out and asking him about his motives wanting a real marriage with her then again by admitting she still wasn't certain about them.

And, while it hurt that the affection combined with the support he'd lavished on her hadn't been enough to show her where he stood, he knew words and deeds should be together.

For full impact, one shouldn't be without the other. Especially where they were concerned. Especially considering their contentious beginning.

"You asked me before why I wanted a real marriage with you. I never gave you a solid answer."

Rubbing his thumb over the back of her hand, he marveled at the silky softness of her skin. From the second they'd said their vows, and he'd received tacit permission to touch her at will, he hadn't been able to keep his hands to himself. Even now, when his heart should be hammering in his chest, he was calmly appreciating being able to touch her.

"I didn't give you an answer, not because I thought it was too soon. We were already married. But, because I thought it might be better if I showed you. That my actions could help you understand what you might not believe in my words."

Atarah's watchful gaze never left his face. Her dark brown eyes saw so much—except the blazing sign hovering over his head and shining from his heart. Piercing her with a determined stare, Cyrus could no longer hold the words he'd bitten back and only whispered to her while she slept.

"I wanted a real marriage with you, because I love you, Atarah Lauder. I've been in love with you since long before we said vows to one another. So, yes. I'm over the moon about the possibility of us creating a life together. Because, that. *This*. Is something I only want to do *with you*."

The gentle shake of Atarah's head along with the tears gathering in her eyes, had Cyrus internally scrambling. Had he said too much too soon? Were they happy tears? Was she denying his love?

"But...Cyrus..." Atarah cleared her throat and fell silent again.

The self-control Cyrus exercised deserved recognition, because he wanted to ask every question forming in his mind. If he had to, he'd beg, without shame, for her to give them a real chance. As much as he knew how he felt about his wife, he was just as certain he wasn't alone.

Aside from their physical attraction to one another, and insane chemistry, she'd exposed her feelings far more than she may have realized. A woman like Atarah didn't yield to the dictates of her libido without being emotionally invested. Recalling the passion she displayed when she gave herself to him, there was no way she felt nothing. That she was simply playing along to save face.

"But what, baby?"

The longer she was silent, he grew concerned he'd misread the signals she'd given him. What if he was wrong?

"Before. Before that day in my office. Before the wedding. We butt heads so much... Hell...We still do."

The timbre of her voice revealed her teetering emotions, giving Cyrus hope. Unable to stop himself from touching her, he stroked loose curls from her forehead and leaned closer.

"What does us not agreeing on every subject have to do with whether or not I could love you? We don't share the same brain. Differences of opinion are bound to happen."

"You think I'm stubborn. And I have a smart mouth. And I don't listen..."

"What's your point? You're also, brilliant. Kind. Strong-willed. Beautiful. And sexy." Each attribute Cyrus listed was accompanied by a kiss. From her forehead, to her nose, then each cheek before landing on her lips.

The sheen of tears hovering at the edges of her eyes spilled down her cheeks. Cyrus's fingers were there to catch them and swipe them away. He wasn't wrong. She was there, hovering on the edge.

"Everything you are comes with the package of the woman who I love to distraction. Even when I tried to fight against it."

"Even when you fought me?" Atarah's speech held a slight quiver.

"Even when I fought you and fought *for* you. I loved you then, and I love you now."

The more he said it, the easier the words tumbled from his mouth. However... She hadn't said it in return. He saw it in her eyes. In the tremble of her lips. In her gentle touch where her hands rested on his chest. But she hadn't given him the words.

While he contemplated their absence, Atarah closed the miniscule gap between them, initiating a kiss which poured out the emotions she hadn't given voice to. Opening his mouth to her unspoken request, he gave her control.

Taking it, she pressed against his chest until he leaned back against the cushions and she was straddling his lap. Filling his hands with the rounded globes of her ass, he caressed then squeezed them, tugging her center closer to his hardening length. Having her initiate intimacy felt amazing, but he wanted more than a physical display. He deserved it as much as she deserved to hear it from him.

Reluctantly, he released his hold on her ass and disengaged from their lip lock. When she let out a discontented grumble, he softened the separation with parting kisses. Peeling away the last layer of himself, he stared at her baldly.

"I feel it, baby. But, I need to hear it too."

One corner of Atarah's bottom lip disappeared between her teeth as she stared at him hungrily. Rubbing her back in small circles, Cyrus worked his hands upward until his fingertips grazed the tight, soft curls at her nape. Considering the gentleness in his touch, there was no way she would predict what came next.

Slipping his digits into her thick mane, he fisted them. Not tight enough to cause real pain, but with enough tension to elicit a slight hiss from the sting.

"Stop holding back on me, woman. Give me the fucking words."

Cyrus barely recognized the growling, gritty timbre of his voice. Her eyes widened, and he was certain she saw the blazing heat in his. A sharp gasp preceded the words he demanded falling from her lips.

"I love you, Cyrus Lauder."

"Damn right you do."

Swallowing anything else she might say with a deal sealing kiss, Cyrus delved his tongue into Atarah's mouth tasting the flavor of her love for him. Keeping one hand tangled in her curls, the other traveled down her torso to the curve of her ass.

Her clothes may as well have been breakaway pieces he undressed her so quickly. Atarah gasped when he captured one puckered nipple between his teeth. Keeping her sensitivity in mind, he flicked the bud with the tip of his tongue. The resulting winding grind of her hips pressed her hot pussy against his still covered cock.

Additional warmth invaded the area and his entire body went rigid. Releasing his captive with a retreating suckle, Cyrus peered into Atarah's face.

"Did you just come on me? Did you just spill your lady spunk on my pants instead of my cock?"

Atarah's eyes drooped. Her bottom lip once again fell victim to her teeth. With zero shame, she nodded still apparently caught up in the bliss of her release. When he smacked her bare ass, she had the nerve to grin at him.

"Oh. So, you *really* want me to show you something. Huh?"

Answering the challenge in her response, he shifted her until he could free his aching shaft from the restriction of his garments. With no preamble or warning, he grasped her hips then deposited her slick sweetness directly onto his turgid length.

The heat of Atarah's channel wrapped around Cyrus's thickness, drawing him in deeper, inspiring him to punch his hips upward as he jerked her down onto his length. He took pleasure in the widening of her eyes once he filled her to the brim with his cock. There was not a millimeter of space he didn't occupy within her depths.

"Cy!" Atarah's head rocked back onto her shoulders and her scream went up to the ceiling.

Loving the sound of his name flying from her lips, he began a multi-pronged assault on her senses. His fingers and lips were everywhere at the same time, tasting, teasing...taking her to the brink of release more than once before he finally tipped them both over into the euphoric feeling they'd chased like the coveted prize that it was.

Cyrus's groans and growls mingled with Atarah's moans and sighs as they reached completion with him spilling his seed into her tight channel while her walls gripped his length, milking him for every drop.

# Chapter Twenty

Atarah was seated at her desk in her office at the church going over documents the board received regarding the renovations on the Lloyd property. They'd moved forward with revitalizing the building instead of selling it. It would allow them to expand their outreach.

She couldn't take credit for swaying their decision and neither could Cyrus. Well... She had somewhat nudged them in the right direction by having Iva come over with one of the structural engineers she worked with at her architectural firm. Once the two of them explained the condition of the building wasn't nearly as poor as they'd been told previously, the board members were more inclined to listen to ideas regarding potential outlay of funds to bring it back up to standard.

The phone on her desk rang with an internal call. Pressing the speaker button, Atarah answered the call from Norma.

"Yes, ma'am?"

"Pastor, Brother Amos is here. And, don't forget your appointment."

"Thank you for the reminder. You can send him in."

Atarah reached into the drawer to get her keys from her purse. She'd just located them when Tim Amos opened the door. A church member who owned a car detailing service, he'd been personally picking up her car then getting it cleaned up for more than a year.

"Good morning, Brother Amos." The smile on her face was evident in her voice. Tim returned the sentiment with a broad smile of his own.

"Good morning, Pastor Cox."

"Lauder. It's Pastor Lauder." Cyrus's correction cut sharply into Tim's greeting.

"Of course, my apologies. Good morning, Pastor Lauder." Tim's head bobbed as he restated his greeting to Atarah before looking at Cyrus. "Brother Lauder. Nice to see you as well."

"Brother Amos." Cyrus's response was as dry as the expression on his face as he stared at Tim, who shifted uncomfortably under his gaze.

"Well... uh. I just came to pick up your car, Pastor. I should have it done and back to you in a couple of hours."

Nodding in agreement, Atarah extended the keys to Tim only to have them plucked from her fingers by her husband.

"Why are you picking up her car?"

Atarah detected the edge of aggression in Cyrus's voice. It took supreme effort for her not to roll her eyes at his antics. The man thought everyone wanted her the same way he did.

"Cyrus, Brother Amos details my car for me whenever it needs it. We have a schedule."

Silently demanding her keys, Atarah held out her hand. Her lips flattened into a pinched line when the irritating man placed them in his pocket rather than give them back to her. Her narrowed gaze did nothing to sway him since he wasn't even looking at her. Instead, he was staring at Tim.

"Brother Tim, we appreciate you stopping by, but it won't be necessary for you to personally pick up and detail the pastor's car any longer. I've got it covered."

Tim's confusion was evident in his expression, however he didn't argue. Instead, he nodded politely to Atarah then bid them both goodbye.

"If you need anything in the future, just let me know."

"We won't. But, thank you for the offer." Regardless of the token *thank you* he tacked onto his statement, it was obvious Cyrus had zero intention of ever calling on Tim's services.

When the door closed behind the other man, Atarah slowly counted to thirty before she looked up at Cyrus. His expression was unrepentant.

"Are you ready to go to your doctor's appointment?"

"Don't do that, Cyrus."

"Don't do what?"

Atarah's narrow eyed glare had next to no effect on her husband. "You know what you're doing. You're acting as if you didn't just march in here and treat Tim poorly for doing what he's been doing for more than a year."

"Oh yeah? And what exactly has he been doing besides trying to get in good with *my wife*?"

Even though she'd known the accusation was coming, Atarah still rolled her eyes. Crossing her arms over her middle she shook her head.

"Cyrus, why would he need to get in good with me? What will happen if he does? I'll pray for him a little harder? What?"

"Baby, prayer is the farthest thing from that man's mind when he looks at you."

"You know what?..." Holding up one hand in surrender, she picked up her purse, slipping the long strap over her shoulder. "I don't have the bandwidth to deal with your delusions this morning."

Stepping into her space, Cyrus pressed his hard body against hers. She had to remind herself she wasn't happy with him when she wanted to melt against his heat as his fingers found their way into the hair at her nape.

"I'm not delusional. I'm observant. Tim Amos isn't driving over here to personally pick up your car for detailing simply because he wants to be nice to the church pastor. Just like Sister Hilda didn't crochet that huge blanket for you because she's a nice woman. Both of them would slide into my spot if you gave them the tiniest encouragement. It's just good for them you don't treat them any differently than anyone else."

Atarah's brain was going to rattle in her skull if she shook her head any harder at Cyrus's outlandish claims.

"Cy... While I appreciate how desirable *you* find me. Everyone isn't into me like that. We both grew up in the church. We've both seen the things people do for the ministers who lead them."

It was good she'd said all she'd intended to say, because Cyrus's lips landed on hers with the last word she uttered. The kiss stole her thoughts since her words weren't available. Tapering off with a few pecks, her husband stared at her with his lust-filled cognac gaze.

"And you call me delusional because I see what you can't. I know how people get when it comes to their pastor. However, I'm right about those two and now they both know that I know. They also know I'm not putting up with their shit. You might be their pastor. But you're my *pastor*."

The different inflection he placed on the word projected his meaning more clearly than the pelvic tilt reminding her of his thickness pressed against her. He was well and truly going to ruin that word for her. As usual, his use of the title in that tone of voice elicited a Pavlovian response to her center. Closing her eyes against the heat in his, Atarah took a beat to get herself together to meet his gaze once more. She was almost so drawn into his thrall she nearly missed something he'd said.

"Did you just say, now they both know? What do you mean by that, Cyrus?"

Again, with absolutely no remorse, her husband informed her of the *gentle* correction he'd given Hilda Wagner a few Sundays prior when he said she'd held on to Atarah's hand a little too long after service.

"You aren't just delusional, you're certifiable. Cyrus, you can't go around threatening elderly women."

"I don't. And I didn't threaten her. You weren't listening. I gently corrected her, letting her know I didn't appreciate her making advances toward my wife in my face."

Stilling Atarah's movements, when she squirmed in his hold, Cyrus shook his head against the denial hovering on her lips.

"She was. Even if you didn't see it. She wasn't taking my subtle hints. I had to get more direct. Just like if Tim hadn't backed off, I'd do the same with him."

"Wait...that's what you call gentle?" Atarah's jaw dropped. She made a mental note to call Hilda to apologize for Cyrus's heavy-handed behavior.

"Would you prefer if I'd hit him? I don't think it would go over well. I definitely couldn't take that route with Hilda. There are laws and stuff."

Tapping his chest in frustration, Atarah couldn't form a coherent comeback which wasn't just as inappropriate and rude as what Cyrus had done.

"You know what? Let's go. I need to get to my appointment early to fill out paperwork since a few things have changed from the last time I was there."

Accepting the change in subject, Cyrus finally released her. The drive to Atarah's OB/GYN took less than thirty minutes and was filled with their discussion of how their individual days were going so far. They stopped shy of revisiting how Cyrus ran Tim off.

# Chapter Twenty-One

Accompanying Atarah to her doctor's appointment was an eye-opening experience for Cyrus. He considered himself a relatively progressive thinking man, but he'd had no idea of the things women went through when it came to their feminine health.

He'd felt violated the first time he'd had his prostate checked, but at least his doctor had been quick about it. Atarah's legs were lifted in that contraption for far longer than he'd had to lean over the table. And although the doctor was nothing other than professional, Cyrus felt some kind of way about how long she was staring at Rapture—not to mention when she was pressing on the twins during the breast exam.

Cyrus didn't like it. *At all*. But, he was told it was a necessary part of the first prenatal visit. They'd used a clinic to get the initial official test results, which they were told wasn't absolutely necessary since the pregnancy tests they used were considered very accurate.

Atarah had a hard time accepting it because she was adamant her IUD should've worked. Quoting the exponentially low failure rate didn't matter in the face of the positive pregnancy tests. There was also the matter of her not realizing the device had an expiration date. She'd exceeded the window where that low failure rate would apply.

Even with the previous testing at home and the clinic, Atarah had to give another sample when they arrived today for yet another test—which came back as conclusively pregnant. When Dr. Ramirez mentioned performing an ultrasound, Cyrus was relieved they'd made it to a portion of the visit he'd expected. Mainly because it was the one he'd seen on television and in movies. But, he'd also done a little research on what to expect. Although he'd read about the breast and pelvic exams, reality had been decidedly different.

With what looked like an undersized, skinny dildo in her hand, Dr. Ramirez rolled her chair back toward the gap between Atarah's lifted legs. Atarah's grip on Cyrus's hands kept him from actively reaching out to protect her from the thing in the doctor's grasp. He didn't want to snatch his fingers away from her, so he used his words instead.

"Whoa, Doc. What are we doing here? I thought you said this was an ultrasound? Where's the thing that looks like a pricing scanner? What's that?"

Laughter tinged the doctor's response, given with a wide smile. "Don't worry, Mr. Lauder. This is an ultrasound wand. According to her test results, your wife is approximately ten weeks into gestation. At this stage, we perform what we call transvaginal ultrasounds. It's perfectly safe. It allows us the best view of the fetus."

Atarah's thumb rubbed against the side of his hand drawing Cyrus's gaze back to her face.

"Cyrus, it's fine. Let Dr. Ramirez do her job."

Although he knew the best way to get answers was to ask questions, Cyrus took his wife's advice and clamped his mouth shut. It didn't stop him from keeping a watchful eye on the doctor as she put some kind of jelly on the dildo wand before inserting. The way Atarah flinched had him glaring at the woman before Atarah squeezed his fingers to get his attention again.

Mouthing, "I'm fine." She pointed toward the monitor where a grainy black, gray and white image was displayed. With a few taps to the keyboard, the image became clearer.

"Aaand...there's our little bean." Dr. Ramirez moved the pointer to the tiny, oddly shaped olive surrounded by darkness.

Struck into silence by the first view of their child, Cyrus could only stare at the screen while the doctor clicked around. He barely heard her as she commented on the size and other benchmarks she expected to see.

He had to blink. Hard. A few times to clear his eyes then pay attention to things she said. When Atarah took the home tests, and he'd seen them lined up on the bathroom counter, he'd thought that was the happiest moment. It was eclipsed by seeing the images on the screen. As soon as Dr. Ramirez passed them their copies, he took out his phone, snapping a picture.

"Are you okay, Cy?"

Atarah's voice reached him from behind the privacy screen where she'd retreated to change back into her clothes.

Glancing up from the slips of photo paper in his hand, Cyrus watched her shadow play across the material as she moved around.

"Yeah... I'm fine. How are you feeling?"

A heavy sigh came from his wife, garnering Cyrus's full attention. Carefully placing the pictures on top of the other documents the doctor had given them, he strode across the room. She rounded the edge of the separator just as he reached it. Walking into his open arms, she laid her head on his chest.

"I'm okay... Filled with awe... A little scared. No scratch that. A lot scared."

Hugging her to him, Cyrus rubbed circles on her back and lowered his chin to rest on the top of her head.

"I understand. I'm feeling those same things."

They took the moment to sit in their feelings, commiserating on the journey they'd begun together. It was a few minutes before she broke the silence with a statement that pierced the heart of the weight which had settled on him when he realized what he was seeing on the ultrasound monitor.

"We have to do better than they did, Cy. We *have* to."

"We will, baby. I promise."

Despite not allowing it to be a constant topic of conversation, they'd both shared regarding their relationships with their parents and how they'd made it to a point where neither set attended the wedding. Cyrus was certain that if his grandparents were still living, they would've come. But his mother's parents passed on when he was a teen. His father's parents, the one's he'd inherited Lauder Industries from, had been deceased less than five years. His parents hadn't even attended the funerals because they'd considered the grandparents support of Cyrus and Caleb being of the world as the final straw. Well, his father did. His mother yielded to her husband as head of the household. She wouldn't ever go against him.

Atarah had confessed much of the same. She'd lost one set of grandparents by the time she'd graduated from college. The others... Her father's parents held to the same beliefs they'd instilled in their son. So, they'd cut contact with her when she wouldn't walk away from her calling.

It was very cultish. The way their parents viewed faith and religion. Cyrus considered them both exceptionally lucky they were able to escape it. It was amazing to him that Adina had been able to do it. Her re-entry into Atarah's life had brought the discussion to the forefront, especially since the sisters had been making a concerted effort to get to know one another again.

"Okay, folks. I think we're all set for today." The nurse entered the room with a few additional papers in her hand along with a few pamphlets.

Turning toward the woman, Cyrus reluctantly released his wife. Smiling broadly at them, the nurse went through a brief recap of what the doctor told them. As she walked to the door to lead them to the scheduling and payment window, she kept up a light stream of conversation.

"Please don't forget. If you have any questions between now and your next appointment, you can reach out via the patient portal. We monitor the messages; so, we can get back with you pretty quickly."

"Thank you. We appreciate it." Giving the nurse her patented preacher smile, Atarah placed the documents in her purse.

Once they were completely done, Cyrus suggested lunch to which Atarah readily agreed. Her appetite had taken another turn. She hadn't had the same sensitivity to smells as she had even a few weeks prior. He was happy to see it, because he didn't think pregnancy was supposed to cause weight loss, and Atarah had lost almost ten pounds before her appetite returned.

And it had returned with a vengeance. Case in point was the way she was staring at his burger while she placed a bite of her chicken breast smothered in gravy into her mouth.

"Would you like a bite?" Cyrus tipped the sandwich in her direction.

"No. I'm fine." Dropping her eyes to her plate, she moved her fork around to mix the sour cream, cheese and bacon bits together in her baked potato.

Her words said she was fine, but her expression said she wanted his burger. Instead of arguing or contradicting her, Cyrus picked up his knife then cut his burger in half.

Placing the side he hadn't bitten off onto her plate, he smiled as her eyes widened with joy at his offering.

"Thank you, baby! You didn't have to do that."

"You're welcome. Don't worry about it. You just keep baking my bun in your oven and we'll call it even."

She was so enamored with the first bite of the juicy bacon cheeseburger she didn't bother to reply to his comment. Cyrus happily watched her consume the half a burger he'd given her along with the food she'd ordered.

He would've handed over the rest or ordered her another if it's what she wanted. He was just pleased she was eating something other than crackers and dry bread. This was going to be an interesting pregnancy, but he was looking forward to the ride and already planning for a possible repeat performance. Although he didn't tell his wife that bit of information.

# Chapter Twenty-Two

The electronic ringing from her cellphone pulled Atarah from the best sleep she'd had in weeks. As her pregnancy progressed, she was finding sleep came at the oddest times and not always when she was in bed at night.

Reaching one hand from beneath the covers, she slapped it around forgetting that she was cuddled next to Cyrus on his side of the bed. The only thing her hand encountered was the plush softness of the duvet cover. Grumbling, Cyrus stretched over her, grabbed the phone, placing it into her hand.

As he settled back against the pillows, she swiped the screen then put the device to her ear.

"Hello."

"Pastor Lauder!"

The frantic pitch of Miss Carolyn's voice put Atarah on high alert. Rolling to a sitting position in the bed, she cleared the sleep from her eyes.

"Miss Carolyn? What's wrong?"

Atarah felt Cyrus sit up behind her and the light flickered on, but she didn't look around.

"There's a fire at the second site. It's…" A sob obscured the rest of Carolyn Moss's words.

Flipping the covers back, Atarah left the bed heading to her closet. As she went, she talked to Carolyn trying to keep her calm while getting as many details as possible. By the time she'd assured Carolyn that she'd be there soon, Cyrus was dressed and standing in the doorway to the bathroom waiting for her.

He had her toiletries lined up for her to quickly get herself together. While she did so, she filled him in on what she'd gathered from Carolyn.

"There was a fire at the second Gentle Hands location. From what I could gather from Carolyn, one of the ladies went out somewhere. Somehow her abuser tracked her, then followed her back. When he couldn't get access to her and no one would give him information confirming she was there, he left. Only he came back a few hours ago."

Meeting Cyrus's gaze in their reflection in the mirror, Atarah saw the way his jaw clenched. She knew it was costing him to remain silent, so she quickly relayed the rest of the information.

"He tossed Molotov cocktails setting the fire, then waited outside to try to catch her when they evacuated. They'd already moved her to another location. So, she's safe."

"What about him? Because I see where this is going, and *you* won't be going anywhere near that place if he's still roaming around."

Finishing with her hair, Atarah turned around, placing her hands on Cyrus's chest. "They caught him. He's in custody. But I wasn't going to the second site."

Cyrus cocked one eyebrow, prompting Atarah to amend her statement. "Okay. I didn't plan to be there long. We need to call a few of the brothers to drive the church vans over there to meet us. Then, I was going down to the Lloyd house to make sure it's opened up and ready as much as it can be right now.

Those poor souls will need some place to lay their heads while the damage is assessed. It's a good thing we're done with enough of the renovations to be able to help them."

Nodding grudgingly, Cyrus stepped away. He met her in the bedroom with her shoes in one hand and her purse in the other. The life of a full-time pastor could be hectic when it came to serving the needs of their congregation. Up until tonight, there had been phone calls and hospital visits, but nothing too emergent.

However, Atarah was pleased with the way her husband stepped up to support her that night. He was on his phone calling people to action with her as he drove her to the Gentle Hands second site. He even suggested reaching out to a few other members of the clergy to lend a hand if there wasn't enough space at the Lloyd building. Cyrus even called Caleb who met them not long after they arrived.

The entire time they were at the site of the fire he was either right by her side or standing slightly away as she talked to the residents who weren't comfortable around men. He and Caleb even stood as human shields to keep the news and people with cameras from getting clear views of the residents while they were being escorted away in the early morning light.

The firefighters had remained on sight for hours dousing the flames while the police were present keeping spectators behind barricades. The fire spread to the structures on either side of the shelter; so, those residents had to be evacuated as well. So, it was a good thing Cyrus had suggested calling the other churches. There were many people who would require temporary homes and assistance.

By the time the sun was fully in the sky, they were at the Lloyd building located slightly down the block from Harmony Haven. The last person had been given a room, bedding and fresh clothes. Members of the kitchen committee were onsite to help feed them.

Their presence made Atarah proud as well as happy she'd convinced them to start the ministry. It was definitely one of the good holdovers from her Baptist upbringing. Harmony Haven had gifted people in their congregation with the time and desire to serve others in that capacity.

"It's time to go home now."

Cyrus didn't ask. The hand he placed at her back offered no room for argument. Caleb, who hadn't cracked one joke fell into step on the other side of her as they took the short walk back to where he'd parked at the church.

His goal to get her home was delayed by the appearance of two news vans at the front of the church. Groaning internally, Atarah was pleased at least they were in front of the church and not the building where the vulnerable residents were being housed. Since they hadn't had the official opening of the location, it appeared the outlets had simply shown up to the place they expected to find her. Being that it was Sunday morning, it was a good guess.

"You know you don't have to talk to them, right?" Cyrus's fingers flexed against her back and his body stiffened next to her.

"I know, but if I don't, they might seek out and find Carolyn. It's better if I give them a sound bite, praise the other ministers who showed up to help. I can steer the conversation away from where people will be housed in the interim."

While they'd been able to house more than half of the group, Atarah had no intentions of releasing that information. As far as she was concerned the best way to keep them safe was to control the narrative. Which was why the members she called to assist were a carefully selected group who could be counted on to respect the need for anonymity of the persons they were helping.

"Reverend Cox."

"Lauder." Atarah corrected the young man approaching her with a camera attached to a tripod and a microphone.

"Excuse me. Reverend Lauder. Do you have a moment to talk about the fire this morning and why you were there?"

Pasting a pleasant expression on her face, Atarah approached the reporter. By the time he was set up, the young lady from the other vehicle had her camera in position. She was also ready to volley questions as well. Standing before them with Cyrus and Caleb behind her, Atarah answered their questions.

After fifteen minutes, Cyrus called an end to the interviews. The adrenaline had worn off and fatigue was setting in. So, Atarah didn't utter a word of protest when he shut things down. The over eager reporter attempting to continue with his questions received a fierce warning glare, making him fall back.

"I said we're done here." The gritty rumble of his voice was the incentive prompting both reporters to cut their feeds without even taking the time to do their recaps.

Once Atarah was seated in the passenger seat of the vehicle, exhaustion hit her in a massive wave. They'd barely made it out of the parking lot before sleep took her. She was nudged awake when they made it home. Atarah made it two steps before Cyrus swept her into his arms taking her to their bedroom.

She was on autopilot as he bathed her in the shower, put her to bed wrapping his arm around her, and holding her as she drifted off.

# Chapter Twenty-Three

The next few days Cyrus went about his normal routine. On Thursday, his mind drifted back to Sunday afternoon. The assistant pastors took care of the service so Atarah could rest. Once she awakened from her much-needed nap, they'd eaten the food he'd had delivered then watched football together. He laughed at her disagreeing with Denzel Reyes as he talked about pros and cons of the Atlanta offense. But, she was a die-hard fan. So, she wouldn't hear of any talk about her team being outmatched—even when they were.

His watch buzzed reminding him of the time, and he began gathering his things to leave. One of the changes he'd made recently was a shorter work week. Although they still had a few months to go before their little bundle would be introduced to the world, there were still things that needed to be done. Also, Cyrus didn't want the entire burden on his wife.

Although her sister and her best friend/cousin seemed to always be hovering nearby, he wanted to be involved as well. He was all packed up and ready to leave when the door to his office was flung open. Looking up, he saw Caleb standing in the doorway looking as if he'd seen something he couldn't quite wrap his mind around.

"Caleb? What's wrong."

Instinctively, Cyrus checked his phone to make sure the ringer wasn't off causing him to miss a call. Walking toward his silent brother, he tried to read the expression on his face to determine what could've happened. Caleb didn't look frightened, but his expression didn't scream, *joy,* either. When Cyrus was a few steps away, he placed a hand on Caleb's shoulder.

"Bro? What's going on?"

"I'm not sure. I just know she's here."

Looking past Caleb's shoulder, Cyrus didn't see anyone other than their executive assistant sitting at her desk.

"Who's here, Caleb? I don't see anyone other than Jill out there."

"No. Not there. In the lobby."

Caleb still hadn't said a name, but seeing that his brother was still processing, Cyrus didn't want to push too hard. He knew of very few people who could rattle Caleb Lauder.

"Who's in the lobby, Caleb?" The second he asked the question, the answer appeared in his mind like a blazing sign. He and his brother spoke at the same time.

"Mom."

Their mother was in the front lobby of Lauder Industries. The mother they hadn't seen face-to-face in almost twenty years. Their last encounter had been at Caleb's college graduation. Once he and his brother both admitted they would be accepting the roles offered to him at their grandfather's company, their parents washed their hands of them.

"Why is she here? Is dad with her?" Regardless of if he thought Caleb had the answer, Cyrus asked anyway.

"I don't know. I don't think so. I was on my way back to my office when Jill was taking the call from the receptionist."

Cyrus looked toward their completely oblivious assistant, then back to his brother. Guiding Caleb out of his office, Cyrus pulled the door closed.

"I guess there's only one way to find out."

As much as he didn't want their family business on display, he didn't ask Jill to have their mother escorted to their offices. Instead, Cyrus strode out of their suite heading toward the main lobby. When they reached the reception desk, their mother was seated in one of the visitor's chairs. With her arms folded across her slim waist, she was looking around as if she thought the walls had eyes and ears.

The second she saw them approaching, she hopped up from the seat like a woman much younger than her sixty years. The eyes she'd given he and Caleb were alight as she approached them.

"Cyrus, Caleb."

Her fingers flexed as if she was struggling to restrain herself from using them to brush their hair away from their foreheads the way she used to do when they were little.

"Mother."

The formality in Cyrus's reply caused the light in her eyes to dim slightly.

"I know it's been a long time. And I didn't call first..." Their mother looked down like she was searching for the words in the tile flooring beneath their feet.

Finally, she looked up again. "I was hoping we could talk. I left your father. I'm not going back."

A feather could've knocked Cyrus over when the weight of his mother's words filtered the hurt clouding vision of her. When their father was at his worst, she never even spoke against him, let alone hinted that she would do anything other than stand beside him. Yet she'd left him.

"Why?"

It would've been prudent to find a private place to talk, however Cyrus's feet were rooted to the floor. They wouldn't allow him to move without answers. His mother's brow wrinkled.

"Why? Why what?"

"Why did you leave him? Why do you want to talk now? It's been almost twenty years."

Tears glistened in her eyes, sending a ping to Cyrus's heart, but he held firm. Caleb stood beside him silently allowing Cyrus to lead. Although they both knew the reason she'd gone no-contact, Cyrus wanted her to admit it. He needed to hear it.

When he didn't yield to the tears or her pleading expression, she began to speak.

"I saw the two of you. On one of those app things the young people are using on the cellular phone. There was a video of the two of you. And your wife, Cyrus."

Understanding filtered through the words she'd yet to speak, but her mention of Atarah flipped on the light in his mind.

His wife was very noticeably pregnant. Not wanting to assume, Cyrus asked the question sitting between them like a two-ton elephant.

"Are you here because of the baby?"

Tears streamed down his mother's face in earnest. While it tugged at his heart strings, he had to remember his responsibility to his own child. He couldn't expose his offspring to people who he knew would toss them aside as if they didn't matter. He wouldn't put his child through loving someone only to have them turn their back when the child didn't do exactly as they wanted.

"Yes and no." When Cyrus tilted his head at her answer, his mother quickly continued. "Yes, I would like the opportunity to be a part of my grandchild's life, but it's not the only reason I left. In the video, I saw you two together. I saw the way you cared for her and how you protected her.

It made me realize I had no idea where you'd learned to do that. Because it hadn't been the example you'd seen from us. Me and your father. It was a very hard pill to swallow, seeing you two be the good men. Kind. Great men and know we could only take credit for a small amount of that. It was obvious to me you weren't doing those things because people were watching you.

Neither of you. You were doing them because that's who you are as human beings. I no longer wanted to be in a place where I was required to treat you as if you didn't exist."

Her voice had started out thready and tear-filled, but by the end of her confession, it was strong. She swiped at the remnants of the wetness on her face then straightened her shoulders.

"I know it's a lot to ask. I'm not expecting you to immediately open your lives to me." Her gaze pinged between them as she spoke. "I'm just hoping. Praying. That the two of you will give me a chance to get to know you. And maybe. In time. I'll earn the opportunity to meet my daughter-in-law and my grandchild."

Cyrus would be lying if he said he hadn't missed his mother. He had. It had taken years and more than a few therapy sessions to realize she hadn't protected them from their father more because she couldn't. She didn't know how. Abraham Lauder was all she knew. She'd left her parents at barely eighteen to marry him. Cyrus was born exactly nine months later.

She had no power in their union. So, her leaving, being there at Lauder Industries, taking the first step to trying to mend their relationship was huge. Without discussing it with Caleb, he knew his brother was on the same page, Cyrus offered a small concession.

"Why don't we start with lunch?"

"Yeah, Cyrus is paying."

Stepping around Cyrus, Caleb wrapped his mother in a hug prompting a new round of tears as she clung to him. When he released her, Cyrus opened his arms in invitation. He had no idea if any of this would work out, but he was willing to try.

"Cyrus?"

His wife's voice pulled him away from comforting his quietly sobbing mother. With wide eyes, he observed the concern in her features as she approached them. He'd hoped to discuss things with her prior to making any introductions. Atarah had removed the option with her unscheduled visit.

Turning their mother around, he felt Caleb move to her other side as Cyrus extended his arm to Atarah. She didn't need further invitation. She stepped closer with her gaze on him searching his face for the answers to her unspoken questions.

"Sweetheart, this is my mother Lydia. Mom, this is my wife Atarah. Reverend Atarah Lauder."

His mother's tears began anew when Atarah replied politely to the introductions then accepted the tentative hug. Amidst the tears she lavished praise on both Cyrus and Caleb.

"You boys are such good men. And Cyrus, marrying a pastor..." Cupping the side of his face, she gave his beard two soft taps. "I'll have to teach you about the diplomacy of being the first spouse."

Caleb's chuckles grew to outright laughter at the stricken expression on Cyrus's face. Atarah didn't help things by hiding her laughter behind her hand. Seeing as she was completely serious with her offer, their mother's face scrunched in confusion.

"What? That's not what they call it now?"

While Cyrus glared at him, Caleb slipped an arm around their mother's shoulders. "That's exactly what they call it, Mom. Cyrus just has a thing about being called a first lady."

The squeeze around his waist from Atarah pulled Cyrus's thoughts away from bopping his brother's head. Their mother's sincerely befuddled reply came softly as Caleb led her toward the doors leading to the parking garage. Falling into step, but lagging behind them, Cyrus leaned down to accept the kiss Atarah offered with her upturned lips.

"Don't worry, baby. I know you aren't first lady material. But you'll always be my first man."

"Damn right I will."

Capturing her lips again, he placed one hand on her protruding belly with the other at her nape. Backing her into the nearest wall, he poured his love and appreciation into the kiss.

"Hey, you two. Knock that off. We're hungry."

Caleb's interruption pulled them apart.

"You really need to work on this habit you have of kissing me when we can't be assured privacy." Atarah smiled against his lips, giving him one last peck before pulling away completely.

"Who says I give a shit about privacy?" Cyrus shot back with a gleam of mischief in his eyes.

"Cyrus Lauder!"

Atarah's incredulous expression said at least one major piece had fallen into place in her mind. Refusing to apologize, he pilfered one last kiss before taking her hand then following his brother and mother into the parking structure. There was no going back. She was his, and he was hers. They were forever tangled together.

# Epilogue

The noise in the fellowship hall was loud enough to wake the dead, but Atarah wasn't bothered. It was a celebration. If people couldn't be boisterous at a celebration, when could they be? The congregation had thrown her and Cyrus a surprise baby shower.

Despite the two of them having previously purchased and planned for everything they needed for their little bundle, she wouldn't reject a single gift given to them in love. It was almost exactly a year from the day Celia had *discovered* them kissing in her office. Their lives were now completely different.

Oh, they were still occasionally disagreeing about things in regard to certain expenditures, but they did it privately now. Cyrus had stepped down as president of the church board. Even with the conditions put into place to remove the appearance of conflict of interest, he thought it was best to cede the chair to another member and simply be active in the church in other ways.

Which left him more time to be a helicopter husband as the delivery date for the baby grew closer. Atarah wouldn't complain. Much. Cyrus made her and their family his priority. She couldn't be upset about having someone openly display their love the way he did.

"So, we're gonna meet this little person any day now, huh?" Iva plopped into the empty seat next to Atarah, ghosting her hand over Atarah's ever-expanding belly.

"That's what they say. Officially, I'm not due for another three weeks. But, according to the last sonogram, this little bun is fully cooked and can pop out any time now."

"Are you sure you're not having twins?" Adina lowered herself into the chair on Atarah's other side.

Shooting her a glare, Atarah's lips thinned. "Don't you dare cuss at me like that."

"And in a church..." Iva shook her head making a tsking noise. "You should be ashamed, Addy."

Widening her eyes, Adina lifted her hands in surrender. "What? I'm sorry, but you know you were thinking it too. If it's not twins, this is one big ass baby."

"Addy! Seriously?!" Atarah's attempt to sound stern was eclipsed by the giggles hovering from the expression on her sister's face. It was comical with her rounded eyes and open mouth.

Atarah couldn't really be angry at the assessment. According to Dr. Ramirez, baby Lauder already tipped the scales at slightly over nine pounds. Of the many things Atarah was looking forward to surrounding the birth of her first child, attempting to push a watermelon out of her love box wasn't one of them.

"I get the feeling you two are over here attempting to corrupt my wife."

Cyrus approached the table carrying two plates, each with a small portion of the food from the buffet set up on the other side of the large room. A few of the ladies had come by offering to fix a plate for her, however she'd assured them she was okay.

When her nose wrinkled then she nudged the spinach and artichoke dip with her fork, Cyrus scooped up the plate, sweeping the offensive blob away.

"I see we're back to hating spinach this week."

Scrunching her face, she wasn't able to restrain herself from licking out her tongue at him.

"I've told you about licking your tongue out at me. I'll give you something to do with it."

Simultaneous groans erupted from Iva and Adina as they both stood.

"And that's our cue to move along." Iva looked over Atarah's head at Adina. "Come on, Addy. Let's get some of this cake before it's gone."

At the mention of cake, Atarah's eyes lit up. Cyrus was just lowering himself into the chair beside her when she slanted a glance at him. Peering at her from the corner of his eyes, he released a sigh.

"One piece of cake coming up."

"Lemon cream cheese please. Not the sheet cake." Atarah added her preference as he walked away.

She'd seen Sister Monty enter with two boxes earlier. And, she'd seen more than one person with a plastic wrapped piece of that creamy lemony goodness. At least that part of her appetite hadn't changed. She still loved Sister Monty's pound cake.

Wiggling happily in her seat, Atarah tucked into the food her husband brought her while she waited for him to secure her dessert. A sharp male exclamation had her pausing with a meatball halfway to her mouth. Lowering her fork, her gaze swept around the room to find Cyrus quickly walking away from Dave Bradshaw with a piece of plastic wrapped pound cake over his head.

"Now, brother Dave, you wouldn't want the pastor not to get dessert at her own baby shower would you? Thank you so much for understanding."

Cyrus tossed the words over his shoulder as he cut a quick path through the tables and children playing to get back to Atarah. Her expression had gone from one of shock to outright giggles by the time he made it to her.

"Cyrus Lauder! What did you do?"

"What I had to. By the time I made it to the table there was nothing there but the sheet cake you said you didn't want." Placing the cake next to her plate, he slid an arm across the back of her chair, dropping a kiss on her cheek.

"There was no way in hell I was going to be responsible for you not getting a slice of Sister Monty's pound cake. Not again."

Cradling his face with her hands, Atarah stroked Cyrus's beard while shaking her head.

"You didn't have to literally take food out of someone else's mouth."

"I didn't. He was the only one who hadn't unwrapped his. So, it was still safe."

His commitment to taking her literally only made her want to laugh harder. And it was likely he knew it from the sparkle in his eyes.

"You are something else."

Mirroring her hold on him, his warm palms cupped her face while his fingertips brushed her hairline.

"Yes, but I'm *your* something, Pastor."

"Yes...Yes you are."

Sealing her statement with a kiss, Atarah gave herself over to the love from the man she'd previously thought held no reverence for her, nor her position within the church. A man, who as it turned out, revered her far beyond her wildest dreams.

The cheers erupting in the room pierced their bubble pulling them apart.

"If that's what happens when you bring your wife a piece of cake, maybe I should get myself one of those."

Caleb's glib comment received a few chuckles, but Atarah didn't miss the way he glanced at Adina when he said it. Nor did she mistake her sister's response to his statement. Her eyeroll and teeth sucking weren't fooling Atarah. There was more to what she'd told her between her and Caleb. But, that was a story for another day.

The End

# Let's Keep in Touch!

Want to be in the know about what I'm doing and what's next in my writing journey? Sign up for my monthly newsletter to receive inside information, sneak peaks and excerpts before anyone else.

https://sendfox.com/DarieMcCoy

Is the inside view from a newsletter not enough? To get more, you should join my Patreon or Ream Stories. Tiers start as low as $5 per month. Dependent on your subscription level, you'll receive many perks from reading along as I write, up to receiving customized book boxes.

https://patreon.com/DarieMcCoy

https://reamstories.com/dariemccoy

# Acknowledgments

As with each book I write, there are a multitude of people who helped me bring the characters to life and tell their story with authenticity. So, first, I'd like to thank Pastor Terri. A few years ago, during the pandemic, I mentioned I would be writing a story about a female pastor. You not only enthusiastically agreed to be a resource, when I actually came back after not mentioning it for years, you offered counsel, context, and a pair of eyes to quality check the book for me. I'm infinitely grateful for your help. To my Darlings, Delights, Decadents and Divas, thank you for being a part of my subscription community. Your comments and energy, as you ready along, help me stay motivated. I look forward to our relationship growing. To the team who's always willing to help me sharpen my saw, I appreciate you. I have the best writing partners in everdom, Brianna Q. Price and Niccoyan Zheng. You ladies read my raw words and always keep it real. I don't have enough words to thank you. For anyone I didn't mention by name, know that I sincerely appreciate everything you do for me and the Indie Author community.

# About the Author

Darie McCoy is an award winning independent author of contemporary, interracial, romantic suspense, and paranormal/shifter romance books. A reader first, she enjoys reading books across many genres although romance holds a special place in her heart. Her experience working in a STEM field offers her a unique perspective which she uses in each story she pens.

When she doesn't have her nose in a book or her fingers on the keyboard, Darie enjoys working in her vegetable garden. A serial hobbyist, she also enjoys knitting, sewing, baking and canning. One of her favorite treats to make is salted caramel popcorn. Amongst her friends, she's known to transport the sweet treat in large quantities to share whenever they get together.

Born and raised in the south, Darie stands by the staunchly held southern sentiments that the best tea is sweet tea and college football is life.

# Also by Darie McCoy

## Central Valley Pack Series
Chosen

Healed

## Frost Family Series
For Real

Sano's Queen (A Novella)

Christmas Candy

## Draft Pick Series
Draft Pick Season I: Carver

Draft Pick Season II: Andrei

Draft Pick Season III: Denzel (Kindle Vella)

## Other books/stories
Involuntary

Just Kiss Me (Part of Cupid's Kiss Anthology)

Toad: Sin City MC Oakland

Controlled Desire: Fall of Desire

The Glassmaker's Helper: The Getaway Chronicles

# Other Preacher's Kid Books

Divine Embrace by Michel Prince

No Weapon by L. Loren

Lion's Den by Dahlia Rose

Worshipping Vines by Brianna Q. Price

Divine Intervention by Cereza

Sins and Serenades by J. Nell

Irreverent Devotion by Niccoyan Zheng